BRIAN S. BRADLEY

The Cliche Chronicles

A Whimsical Journey Through the World of Clichés

First edition

This book was professionally typeset on Reedsy.
Find out more at reedsy.com

Contents

Introduction

Never has a phrase been more misunderstood than "raining cats and dogs." People have uttered it for centuries, usually while scurrying indoors during a downpour. Yet, no one has ever actually seen pets tumbling from the sky. It's a cliché; a well-worn expression we use without a second thought. But have you ever wondered where it came from? Or why do we keep using it, despite its absurdity?

Welcome to "The Cliche Chronicles: A Whimsical Journey Through the World of Clichés." This book aims to take you on a journey through the history and evolution of clichés. We'll explore how these phrases have shaped language and culture over time. Along the way, we'll meet renowned writers, poets, philosophers, and everyday people who have used them to make a point, add color, or just fill a gap when words fail.

Clichés are everywhere. They pop up in literature and media, in our daily conversations, and even in the digital realm of social media. They're as common as dirt, yet each carries a story. This book sets the stage to explore their fascinating histories and surprising origins.

Historically, clichés have had quite the journey. They started as fresh and original expressions, only to become overused and predictable over time. The term "cliché" itself comes from the printing world, where it refers to a stereotype or a printing plate used to reproduce the same text repeatedly. Much like these plates, the phrases became repetitive, losing their original charm.

Why do clichés matter? They serve as communicative shortcuts, quickly conveying ideas without much effort. Yet, they can also stifle creativity, acting as barriers to fresh thought. Understanding clichés helps us appreciate the balance between ease of communication and the pursuit of originality.

Throughout this book, you'll find a narrative thread that ties together cultural significance, humor, and modern adaptation. We'll explore how clichés have been used in different contexts and how they continue to evolve in our ever-changing world. You'll find stories from history and personal anecdotes that shed light on their enduring presence.

I invite you to reflect on your use of clichés. Are they just fillers in your conversations, or do they hold any significance? This journey will challenge your perceptions and, hopefully, enhance your appreciation of language.

On a personal note, clichés have always intrigued me. I recall a time when I tried to impress a date by quoting Shakespeare, only to realize later that my choice of words was the Elizabethan equivalent of "been there, done that." This experience showed me the power and pitfalls of clichés, sparking a lifelong interest in their impact on communication.

The book is organized into chapters that trace the journey of clichés from their historical roots to their modern implications and future speculations. Each chapter delves into different themes, offering insights and stories that bring clichés to life.

So, dear reader, I encourage you to join me on this adventure with an open mind. Be ready to explore, challenge, and perhaps even change your understanding of clichés. By the end of this journey, I hope you'll see these phrases in a new light, appreciating their hidden power and potential for creativity.

Let's dive into this whimsical world, where the mundane becomes magical, and the familiar turns into a fascinating tale of language and lore.

Chapter 1: The Birth of Clichés

Ever encountered the saying "as old as the hills"? At first glance, it may appear to be merely another overused expression, yet this cliché harbors deeper significance than one might initially suspect. It serves as a testament to our forebears' exceptional talent for storytelling—a vital skill meticulously handed down through the ages, akin to a cherished family recipe, though arguably, more resilient to the passage of time. Contrary to your great-grandmother's legendary casserole, clichés have not always been met with sighs of exasperation. In the tapestry of early human societies, they acted as a crucial adhesive, facilitating communication in ways that were both deeply meaningful and eminently practical.

The Dawn of Familiar Phrases

Long before books lined shelves and tweets filled our feeds, people relied on the spoken word. The world's first storytellers gathered around flickering fires and spun tales that captivated their listeners. These ancient narrators had a problem, though: how to ensure their stories were remembered and retold. Enter the cliché—those repetitive phrases that made stories stick like honey on a spoon. In the absence of writing, people relied on these storytelling shortcuts, and before you knew it, a whole lexicon of familiar expressions was born. What started as a tool of necessity became the foundation of our linguistic heritage.

In the days of yore, when Wi-Fi was a mere twinkle in humanity's eye, oral traditions were the backbone of society. Tribes depended on repetitive storytelling to pass down important knowledge and cultural values. These stories, told and retold, were filled with phrases that quickly became recognizable. This predictability wasn't just a quirk; it was essential for survival. People used these verbal patterns like mnemonic devices to remember important information, much like tying a string around your finger to remember an errand. The bards and storytellers of the time were the keepers of this knowledge, weaving memory aids into their narratives to ensure that even the most forgetful listener could recall the tale.

Beyond memory, clichés served another crucial role—they bonded communities. Shared phrases were more than just words; they were the verbal threads that connected individuals to a larger tapestry of identity and tradition. When you heard a familiar expression, it was like a secret handshake, a nod of recognition that you were part of something bigger than yourself. In tribal settings, these sayings reinforced communal identity, acting as verbal badges of belonging. Imagine a group huddled together, nodding in agreement as the storyteller recited a well-worn phrase. It was these moments that solidified social bonds and created a sense of unity among diverse groups.

Clichés also played a significant role in breaking down barriers between cultures. As different tribes and communities crossed paths, these recognizable phrases served as linguistic bridges, enabling communication without the need for a common language. Much like how a smile or a nod can convey understanding, clichés provide a way for people to connect across cultural divides. They were the original translators, encapsulating complex ideas in simple, universally understood terms. This ability to communicate across cultures was invaluable, allowing for the exchange of ideas, goods, and stories.

Reflect and Relate: Your Clichés

Think about the clichés you use daily. Which ones have become second nature, slipping into conversation like old friends? Consider their origins and how they might have helped people connect in the past. Share a few with friends or family, and see how these phrases resonate with them. You might find that even the most overused expressions have a history worth exploring.

As we continue to explore the world of clichés, remember these early storytellers who laid the groundwork for our modern expressions. Their tales, though ancient, are the seeds from which our language has grown. So next time you catch yourself saying, "better late than never," take a moment to appreciate the rich tapestry of history that phrase carries with it.

Echoes of Antiquity: Clichés in Ancient Texts

Picture this: you're a scribe in ancient Mesopotamia, diligently copying texts by the flickering light of an oil lamp. As you ink the papyrus, some phrases start to feel oddly familiar. These aren't just any words—they're the precursors to what we now call clichés. Ancient texts, whether religious scriptures or epic tales, brimmed with repeated motifs. In religious writings, such as the Psalms or the Rig Veda, certain expressions appeared over and over, like a refrain in a catchy song. Repetition wasn't just about making things stick in the minds of those who couldn't read; it was about reinforcing beliefs and values, cementing them in the collective consciousness. It was less about "an eye for an eye" and more about hammering home the moral lessons that shaped civilizations.

Leap forward to the grand arenas and bustling forums of ancient Rome, where orators stood, toga-clad, before eager audiences. These speakers knew the power of a well-placed cliché. They employed these expressions not just for their memorability but for their persuasive power. In an age where rhetoric was king, clichés were the jewels in the crown. Roman orators like Cicero were masters of this, using familiar phrases to sway public opinion and rally the masses. They understood that a phrase repeated often enough could become a mantra, a rallying cry that united people in a common cause. Clichés were the ancient world's version of a political slogan, simple yet powerful enough to linger in the listener's mind long after the speech had ended.

As these ancient texts made their way across cultures and languages, clichés were carried along, much like stowaways on a ship. The translation of these works played a crucial role in their preservation. Take the Bible, for example. As it was translated from Hebrew to Greek, Latin, and beyond, many of its repetitive phrases were maintained, becoming part of the linguistic fabric of countless cultures. The impact of these translations can't be overstated. They ensured that phrases like "a land flowing with milk and honey" would be recognized and used by people far removed from the original context. Greek and Latin texts, too, found their way into other languages, bringing with them a treasure trove of expressions that would echo down through the ages.

Fast forward to today, and you'll find that many of our modern clichés can be traced back to these ancient roots. When you say something is "all Greek to me," you're tapping into a phrase that has been around since medieval times, originating from the Latin "Graecum est; non potest legi" (It's Greek; it cannot be read). Ancient clichés have morphed and evolved, yet they remain embedded in our language, a testament to their enduring power. They connect us to the past, reminding us that while the world changes, the way we express ourselves often remains surprisingly familiar.

Case Study: Translating Timelessness

Consider the phrase "to err is human." This saying has its roots in Latin, "errare humanum est," and has been preserved through countless translations. Reflect on how this expression has remained relevant, illustrating the timeless nature of certain clichés. Think about how other phrases you use daily might have similarly ancient origins and how they continue to resonate across languages and cultures.

As we explore the echoes of antiquity, it's clear that clichés have played a vital role in shaping not just language but the very way we communicate and connect across time and space. They're the threads that weave our linguistic heritage, linking us to the voices of those who came before, and reminding us that the more things change, the more they stay the same.

From Shakespeare to Dickens: Literary Clichés Unveiled

Ah, Shakespeare and Dickens, those titans of literature, masters of the quill, and unwitting architects of some of the most notorious clichés. It seems hardly fair to call them out for something they did so well. But here we are, dissecting their contributions to the endless sea of phrases we all know too well. Let's start with Shakespeare, the bard who had a way with words like no other. To say he influenced modern expressions is like saying water is wet.

Shakespeare had a knack for coining phrases that stuck, phrases like "to be or not to be," which, despite its existential weightiness, has been reduced to a catchphrase for indecision. Who would have thought that one man's musings on life and death could become a staple of pop culture? Yet, that's the power of Shakespeare. His words have seeped into the fabric of everyday language, popping up in conversations, sitcoms, and even memes.

Charles Dickens, a figure often linked with the somber narratives of Victorian England, made an indelible mark on the lexicon of everyday language, a fact that might astonish those who pigeonhole him into a niche of gloomy tales. Dickens possessed an exceptional ability to observe societal peculiarities and translate them into unforgettable prose. Consider the phrase "a penny for your thoughts," a charming invitation to delve into someone's private musings for the modest price of a coin. This expression, teeming with Dickensian charm, encapsulates his acute awareness of the human condition. His narratives, set against the backdrop of a society in the throes of the Industrial Revolution, captured the zeitgeist of an era marked by profound social and economic transformation. The characters Dickens crafted were not merely fictional beings but embodiments of the era's shifting values and norms, their dialogues mirroring the evolving societal landscape. Through the serialized publication of his works, which were also performed in public readings, Dickens' ingenious phrases permeated the collective consciousness, weaving themselves into the fabric of everyday speech. Dickens' literary prowess lay not only in his storytelling but in his capacity to mirror the complexities of Victorian society. His tales, rich with the intricacies of human life amidst industrial change, offered a lens through which to view the contrasts and contradictions of the time. By embedding these observations in his language, Dickens ensured that his phrases resonated deeply, transcending the pages of his books to become fixtures of common discourse. His ability to distill the essence of his era into accessible language is a powerful demonstration of literature's role not just as a reflection of society but as a force capable of shaping it. As a result, Dickens' contributions to the vernacular endure, his expressions gaining a new lease of life as they transitioned from literary quotations to spoken words, cherished and repeated by generations far removed from the cobblestone streets of Victorian England.

The transition of these literary clichés into common usage wasn't a deliberate act but rather a natural progression, much like the way a catchy song becomes an earworm. It was the theater, with its mix of drama and spectacle, that propelled Shakespeare's phrases into the limelight, while Dickens' serialized novels, devoured eagerly by the masses, ensured his expressions became household staples. Public readings further popularized these phrases, as audiences delighted in the language that seemed to capture their own experiences and emotions.

Literary clichés often serve as mirrors of the society in which they were born. Shakespeare's work, for instance, captured the nuances of Elizabethan England, a time when the English language was experiencing a renaissance of sorts. His plays reflected the social, political, and moral questions of the day, embedding them in words that have endured for centuries. Similarly, Dickens' writings offered a window into the complexities of Victorian life, from the struggles of the working class to the opulence of the upper crust. His use of language highlighted the stark realities and contradictions of his time, making his clichés all the more resonant.

As these phrases trickled down from the pages of literature to the tongues of the masses, they gained new life. They became shorthand for complex ideas, accessible to everyone, whether a scholar studying Elizabethan drama or a child reading "A Christmas Carol" for the first time. These literary clichés bridged gaps, connecting people across classes and generations, all thanks to the unintentional foresight of two of history's most celebrated writers. And so, the words of Shakespeare and Dickens continue to echo, as relevant today as they were then, a testament to the timeless nature of truly great writing.

Philosophical Repetitions: The Thinkers' Influence

When you hear "I think, therefore I am," you're probably picturing a serious philosopher in a dark study, pondering life's great mysteries. But did you know that this phrase, coined by René Descartes, is one of the most enduring clichés ever? It's a testament to how philosophers have a knack for creating phrases that stick around, much like gum on a shoe. With their grand ideas and complex concepts, these thinkers have contributed some of the most memorable sayings to our cultural lexicon. Their words often start in the lofty realms of academia before trickling down into our everyday chatter, where they live on as clichés. Take Plato, for example. Like the famous "Allegory of the Cave," his allegories delve into profound themes about reality and perception. Yet, his insights are now distilled into simple phrases that easily convey complex ideas. These sayings help us navigate the murky waters of reality, offering clarity in a world that often feels like a shadowy cave.

Nietzsche, on the other hand, gave us aphorisms such as "That which does not kill us makes us stronger." It's a phrase you'd likely hear in a gym or during a motivational speech, yet it stems from Nietzsche's deep philosophical musings on strength and adversity. His ability to encapsulate life's trials in a few striking words has made his ideas accessible to those far removed from the world of philosophy. These philosophical clichés have a way of embedding themselves into our consciousness, simplifying complex thoughts into nuggets of wisdom that resonate across time.

The beauty of these philosophical clichés lies in their simplicity. They reduce intricate ideas into bite-sized pieces that anyone can digest, embodying truths that feel as relevant today as they did centuries ago. Consider the phrase "The unexamined life is not worth living," attributed to Socrates. It's a call to introspection, urging us to ponder the more in-depth questions of existence. This classic saying continues to inspire self-reflection in a world that's often too preoccupied with the surface. Such philosophical clichés endure because they address timeless existential questions, bridging the gap between the abstract and the tangible, offering guidance in life's chaotic journey.

In today's world, these philosophical sayings have found new life in the pages of self-help books and motivational talks. They serve as the backbone for advice on living a fulfilled life, acting as philosophical anchors in a sea of self-improvement rhetoric. When you hear someone quote Descartes or Nietzsche, it's not just a nod to their genius; it's an acknowledgment of the enduring relevance of their insights. These clichés have been woven into the fabric of modern thought, influencing how we perceive ourselves and the world around us. They remind us that, despite the passage of time, certain truths remain constant, echoing through history and into our daily lives.

In the ebb and flow of daily chatter, it's not uncommon to lean on these philosophical clichés, often without a flicker of recognition of their deep historical roots. These phrases serve as the ultimate linguistic bridges, effortlessly carrying profound insights across the vast expanse of time and thought in just a handful of words. Imagine, for a moment, you're lost in thought about the vast tapestry of existence or quietly reflecting on the contours of your inner life. It's in these instances that you're not merely mulling over personal quandaries; you're engaging in an age-old philosophical discourse. This is a dialogue that stretches back through the centuries, linking you to the intellectual titans like Plato and Nietzsche. These clichés, though simple in form, are potent in meaning, acting as conduits for a complex exchange of ideas that have been percolating since antiquity. Next time you catch yourself pondering the greater mysteries of life or in the throes of introspection, recognize this act as your contribution to a conversation that has been unfolding for millennia. It's a dialogue that transcends time and place, facilitated by the enduring power and elegance of the philosophical cliché.

Clichés in Folklore and Mythology

Imagine sitting by a crackling fire, listening to tales of cunning foxes and brave heroes, each story steeped in the familiar rhythms of folklore. These tales, with their archetypal characters and recurring themes, have been with us longer than we can remember. In every corner of the globe, from the icy plains of Siberia to the sun-baked deserts of Africa, these stories share a common thread: the use of clichés. Folklore is rife with these well-worn expressions, from the trickster foxes of European tales to the wise old tortoises of African lore. They serve as both a guide and a warning, whispering age-old truths about human nature and the world around us.

These clichés are more than just storytelling shortcuts; they're moral compasses disguised as bedtime stories. Aesop, the ancient Greek fabulist, was a master at weaving them into his fables. His tales, like "The Tortoise and the Hare," use familiar themes to teach lessons that resonate even today. Slow and steady wins the race, anyone? Greek mythology also offers a treasure trove of such narratives. Consider the story of Icarus, who flew too close to the sun. It's an ancient warning against hubris, wrapped in the dramatic flair of myth. These tales, with their predictable plots and characters, serve as reminders of the virtues and vices that define human existence. They're like age-old instruction manuals, guiding us on how to live a life of virtue—or at least how to avoid being turned into a cautionary tale.

But how did these stories spread so far and wide? The answer lies in the ancient trade routes, those bustling highways of cultural exchange. Traders and travelers carried these tales, sharing them over campfires and crowded marketplaces. As they moved from one culture to another, the stories adapted, picking up local flavors and new clichés. Imagine a merchant swapping tales over a cup of spiced tea, each story morphing ever so slightly as it crossed borders. This exchange turned local lore into global myths, allowing stories to evolve and thrive in new environments. It's a testament to the power of storytelling that a myth born in Greece could find echoes in the legends of the Far East.

Fast-forward a few centuries, and you'll see these age-old clichés finding new life in modern media. Movies, books, and even video games draw heavily on these mythological themes, reimagining them for contemporary audiences. Consider the countless films that retell the tale of the hero's journey, a narrative structure as old as time. These modern adaptations breathe new life into ancient stories, ensuring their continued relevance in today's fast-paced world. The Marvel superhero films, for instance, are a masterclass in this kind of storytelling. They transform the gods of old into caped crusaders, battling not just villains but the timeless clichés of myth. These modern tales may be wrapped in CGI and special effects, but their core remains the same: a reflection of the enduring power of storytelling.

As you immerse yourself in the latest cinematic epic or page-turning bestseller, pause to acknowledge the lineage of the narratives enthralling you. These mythological clichés, timeless in their wisdom and allure, have traversed centuries, acting as beacons of guidance, education, and a mirror to our collective human journey. They forge a venerable bridge to our ancestry, echoing tales that predate the advent of writing, tales that were whispered around fires and etched in the memories of generations. Moreover, they are not mere relics of the past but dynamic blueprints that continue to inform and shape the stories we craft and cherish today. In this way, they ensure that the essence of our shared tales—our hopes, dreams, fears, and moral dilemmas—remains vibrantly alive, weaving through the fabric of our contemporary narratives and connecting us to the vast tapestry of human experience.

The Evolution of Language: From Oral Tradition to Print

Imagine a world where words weren't just fleeting sounds disappearing into the ether but were captured forever in ink. This shift from oral to written language was like trading in a whisper for a loudspeaker, amplifying the reach and permanence of communication. The invention of the printing press in the mid-15th century was nothing short of revolutionary. Before then, books were painstakingly copied by hand, as tedious as watching paint dry. However, with Johannes Gutenberg's press, texts could be reproduced quickly and accurately, ushering in a new era of information dissemination.

Clichés, those trusty stalwarts of human communication, thrived in this new environment. With the press, the power of the written word expanded exponentially. The language was standardized, making it easier for people across different regions to understand each other. This standardization boosted clichés, ensuring that they were not just local quirks but phrases that could be recognized and understood by a wider audience. As pamphlets and books became more widespread, so did the clichés contained within them. These pamphlets, often filled with religious and political content, were the social media of their day, spreading ideas—and clichés—far and wide.

By the 19th century, newspapers had taken center stage, becoming the primary means of mass communication. These papers, filled with the latest news and gossip, were a breeding ground for clichés. Journalists, ever needing catchy headlines and engaging prose, often relied on clichés to convey familiar ideas quickly and effectively. Expressions like "all the news that's fit to print" and "the pen is mightier than the sword" became popular through repeated use in print, embedding themselves in the public consciousness.

As literacy rates soared, thanks partly to widespread education reforms in Europe, clichés found fertile ground to flourish. People who could read were more likely to encounter and use these phrases, spreading them like wildfire through letters, essays, and personal conversations. Literacy movements aimed at educating the masses inadvertently contributed to the propagation of clichés. The more people read, the more they absorbed these expressions, using them as shorthand in their everyday language.

Fast-forward to today, and we see that the evolution from print to digital media has only accelerated the cliché train. With the internet, clichés spread faster than ever, crossing borders and cultures with the click of a button. Social media platforms are rife with them, turning old expressions into hashtags and viral memes. It's not just about the words any more; it's about how quickly and widely they can be shared.

This historical journey from oral tradition to print and digital media shows how clichés have adapted and thrived. They've moved from campfire tales to printed pages to our screens, proving that while the medium may change, the message remains the same. Clichés continue to connect our past to our present, reminding us of the enduring nature of language and the human need for shared understanding.

As we close this chapter on clichés, it's clear that these phrases, though sometimes dismissed as tired or overused, hold a mirror to our collective history. They capture the essence of human communication, reflecting the desires, challenges, and triumphs of societies across time. In embracing clichés, we embrace a piece of ourselves, a testament to the power of words to transcend time and technology.

Chapter 2: Clichés and Communication

P icture this: you're walking down the street, minding your own business, when you overhear someone say, "It's the best thing since sliced bread!" Suddenly, you're flooded with images of perfectly cut loaves, and you can't help but chuckle. Why? Because clichés have this strange, almost magical ability to resonate with us. These phrases, though predictable, are like the comfort food of language. They're mentally attractive because they wrap our thoughts in familiarity, much like a warm blanket on a cold day. But why do our brains light up at the mere mention of a cliché? Well, it turns out there's some science behind it.

The Psychology Behind Clichés

Clichés effortlessly infiltrate our minds, as seamlessly as a cat navigating through a slightly ajar door. This phenomenon can be attributed to cognitive fluency, an elegant term describing our brain's preference for simplicity and ease. Picture your brain as a teenager with a penchant for the easiest route available—this is precisely how it reacts to clichés. Upon encountering a cliché, the brain doesn't strain or stumble; it relaxes, metaphorically reclining and allowing the familiar phrases to envelop it in comfort. This quality renders clichés irresistibly charming, offering a cognitive shortcut that distills complex concepts into digestible, easily understood nuggets. They streamline decision-making, enabling us to rely on the sturdy scaffold of a cliché, permitting us to agree with "It is what it is," sidestepping the need to delve into exhaustive detail. This process illustrates the brain's fondness for pathways cleared of linguistic underbrush, where meaning is effortlessly gleaned without the toil of parsing novel or intricate expressions.

But clichés aren't just about making things easy on the old gray matter—they pack an emotional punch, too. These phrases are like old friends, evoking memories and feelings that hit you right in the nostalgia. Think about it: when someone says, "Home is where the heart is," you're transported back to cozy nights and familiar faces, even if you're miles away from the place you call home. Clichés have an uncanny ability to trigger emotional responses because they're tied to shared experiences and cultural touchstones. They're the verbal equivalent of a warm hug, offering comfort and connection in a world that can often feel isolated and impersonal. This emotional resonance is why clichés endure, despite their predictability. They remind us of who we are and where we've been, creating a sense of belonging and shared understanding.

In social settings, clichés are the glue that holds conversations together. They are the common language we all speak, regardless of age or background. When you drop a cliché into a chat, it's like throwing a universal Frisbee—everyone can catch it, and it keeps the conversation flowing. They help build community, much like that one friend who always knows how to defuse a tense situation with a well-timed joke. Whether you're at a family gathering or a work meeting, clichés bridge the gaps between us, providing a shared vocabulary that everyone understands. This is why they're often used in group settings, where the goal is to connect and communicate efficiently. You might roll your eyes at the overuse of "teamwork makes the dream work" during office meetings, but it gets the point across.

Reflection Exercise: Your Personal Cliché

Reflect on the clichés that pepper your conversations. Are they true extensions of your personality, or merely habitual placeholders that fill the voids in dialogue? Challenge yourself: in your next interaction, replace a commonly used cliché with a phrase that's uniquely yours and observe the outcome. Was the exchange more captivating? Did it ignite a richer, more nuanced conversation? This experiment serves as an engaging method to assess the interplay between the comfort of familiar expressions and the invigorating spark of originality in our speech. Clichés, those reliable staples of communication, transcend their reputation as mere repetitive phrases. They streamline our interactions, stir emotions, and weave threads of connection among us. Therefore, when you find yourself defaulting to a well-worn cliché, pause and consider: at times, the most profound sentiments are best conveyed through words that have echoed through countless conversations.

Clichés in Everyday Conversation: A Linguistic Study

Have you ever noticed how clichés sneak into conversations like uninvited guests who somehow make the party better? They're the linguistic equivalent of comfort food. We rely on them when conversation lulls or want to sound like we know what we're talking about. Stroll through any bustling café, and you'll hear clichés flying back and forth like a game of verbal ping-pong. "At the end of the day," "thinking outside the box," and "it is what it is" are just a few of the usual suspects. These phrases pop up so often in our chats that you could almost set your watch by them. They're as frequent as the changing tides and serve a purpose—sometimes more than one.

Clichés often appear where language is meant to build bridges, like workplaces or social gatherings. They're the WD-40 of verbal exchanges, smoothing over awkward silences and greasing the wheels of small talk. If you've ever been stuck in an elevator with a colleague and found yourself saying "same old, same old," then you've witnessed a cliché at work. It's a safe bet that clichés are most at home in these common contexts, where predictability is key. They keep the dialogue moving, ensuring no one is floundering for words. It's like having a trusty Swiss Army knife in your conversational toolkit—always ready, versatile, and dependable.

But here's the kicker: not everyone uses clichés the same way. Take teenagers, for example. They have their trending clichés, often borrowed from the latest TikTok trends or meme culture. Phrases like "that's so sus" or "bet" pepper their interactions, showing how clichés adapt to fit the times. These youthful expressions serve as a social currency, helping teens navigate the complex world of adolescent communication. Meanwhile, older generations may stick to the classics, relying on phrases that have stood the test of time. This difference in usage across age groups reveals how clichés can unite and divide us, acting as linguistic markers of our generation.

Interestingly, the prevalence of clichés can stifle language innovation, but it can also spark new expressions. Cliché fatigue—yes, it's a thing—drives creative minds to seek fresh ways to express the same tired ideas. This quest for novelty has given birth to some of the most delightful idioms and phrases we use today. It's like when you get tired of eating the same sandwich every day, so you throw in a little hot sauce to spice things up. In this way, clichés inadvertently fuel linguistic creativity, prompting people to break away from the norm and invent new ways to communicate.

In the grand theater of conversation, clichés play the understudy role, always ready to step in when the dialogue falters. They keep the verbal ball rolling, ensuring that conversations don't come to a grinding halt. This is where photic communication comes into play—those little exchanges are more about social connection than exchanging information. Clichés excel at this, providing a backdrop of familiarity that fosters interaction. Next time you find yourself nodding to "it is what it is," take a moment to appreciate its role in keeping the conversation alive.

Through the lens of clichés, you can see how language evolves and adapts. They are the comforting old tunes we hum absentmindedly and the springboard for new linguistic adventures. Whether you're using them to bond with a friend or struggling to find something more original to say, clichés are an integral part of our daily dialogues. They are the unsung heroes of communication, ever-present, ever-reliable, and ever-evolving.

Bridging Generations: Clichés as Connectors

Imagine sitting around a family dinner table, where the youngest and oldest generations come together. The conversation might flow seamlessly or hit a few bumps, but one thing's for sure: clichés are the great equalizers. They serve as a linguistic bridge, connecting grandkids with grandparents in a way few other things can. You might hear Grandpa start with a classic "Back in my day," and you're instantly whisked away to a time when gas was a nickel, and walking uphill both ways was an everyday occurrence. This isn't just nostalgia talking—it's the power of clichés as tools for intergenerational communication. They create common ground where age gaps might otherwise cause a conversational chasm. Whether you're an energetic teen or a wise elder, clichés offer a shared language that makes understanding each other easier.

As time ticks on, clichés evolve, shedding their old skins and donning new ones, much like your favorite band trying to stay relevant. Those sayings your parents used? They've likely morphed or stuck around, depending on their staying power. Take "cool beans," for instance—a phrase your mom might have used in high school, which now sounds quaint to your ears. Fast-forward a few decades, and your own "lit" or "savage" might evoke similar eye-rolls from the next generation. It's a linguistic evolution that keeps clichés fresh and relevant, adapting to cultural shifts while maintaining their essence. Parental sayings, too, have undergone this transformation. The once ubiquitous "Because I said so" might now be paired with a digital twist, like "I'll take away your Wi-Fi." It's an evolution that reflects the changing landscape of authority and technology, yet at its heart, it remains the same: a parental power play wrapped in a familiar phrase.

In the familial setting, clichés often masquerade as nuggets of wisdom passed down from generation to generation. They're like those heirloom recipes—tried, tested, and sometimes stale. "Do as I say, not as I do" is a classic example of advice that's both sage and slightly hypocritical. It's the saying parents use when caught in a classic do-as-I-say situation. These phrases impart lessons without the need for a lengthy lecture, offering guidance wrapped in a neat verbal package. Parents wield them like an ancient scroll of wisdom, doling out advice that's simple to remember and even easier to ignore until, one day, you find yourself repeating it to your kids.

Generational language barriers can be as tricky to navigate as assembling flat-pack furniture without the instructions. Miscommunication often sneaks in when you least expect it, especially when different generations speak different dialects. However, shared clichés can serve as a Rosetta Stone, translating the foreign into the familiar. Adapting these phrases to fit modern contexts can help bridge the gap. For instance, while "don't judge a book by its cover" might still hold sway, "don't swipe left too quickly" could be more relatable to today's digital denizens. These adaptations keep the spirit of the cliché alive while making them accessible to new audiences. So, when the generational divide feels as wide as the Grand Canyon, remember that a well-chosen cliché might be the verbal bridge you need.

Clichés continue to evolve, serving as bridges and connectors, transcending the barriers of age and time. They're the secret sauce in the communication recipe, adding flavor and familiarity to conversations across generations. Whether you're the one telling the stories or rolling your eyes, clichés are there, ready to connect and communicate, reminding us all that some things, like words, never truly age.

Clichés in Cross-Cultural Communication

Have you ever tried explaining the saying "the grass is always greener on the other side" to someone who doesn't speak your language? It's like trying to describe the taste of bubblegum—everyone knows it, but pinning it down is tricky. Clichés often feel universal, yet they can trip us up when we cross cultural borders. What sounds perfectly logical in one language might become a head-scratcher in another. Take our grassy cliché, for instance. In Spanish, they might say "el jardín del vecino siempre es más verde" (the neighbor's garden is always greener), but in Japanese, you might hear "のはい" (tonari no shibafu wa aoi), which means the neighbor's lawn is blue. It all boils down to the same idea, but the way it's dressed up varies across the globe.

Clichés can be as slippery as a fish when it comes to translation. They carry layers of meaning steeped in cultural context, so when you try to translate them literally, you might end up with a hot mess. Imagine telling a French friend something is "a piece of cake." You might get a confused look since the French equivalent is "c'est du gâteau," which means the same thing but gets lost in translation without context. These linguistic hurdles can lead to misunderstandings and awkward moments, especially when cultural nuances are missed. It's like playing a game of telephone—by the time the message reaches the last person, it's changed completely. What starts as a simple phrase can morph into something unrecognizable, leaving everyone scratching their heads.

Clichés often reflect the values and norms of a culture, acting as tiny windows into how a society thinks and feels. Consider Japanese sayings, which often emphasize honor and respect. These phrases are more than words; they embody the nation's deep-rooted cultural ideals. Sayings like "るはたれる" (deru kugi wa utareru) meaning "the nail that sticks out gets hammered down," reflect the importance of conformity and harmony. In contrast, American clichés might celebrate individuality, with expressions like "march to the beat of your drum." These linguistic quirks reveal what each culture holds dear, serving as guides to understanding broader societal beliefs. Through clichés, you can glimpse the collective psyche of a people, much like peering through a kaleidoscope to see a colorful array of values and traditions.

Navigating the choppy waters of cross-cultural communication requires a bit of finesse. Using clichés effectively in multicultural settings involves more than just knowing the words; it's about understanding the context and nuances that come with them. Sensitivity is key; sometimes, it's best to swap out a well-worn phrase for something more universally understood. Cross-cultural communication workshops can be a goldmine for bridging these linguistic gaps. They offer strategies for decoding clichés and transforming them into tools for connection rather than confusion. Imagine a group exercise where you practice translating clichés into their cultural equivalents, gaining insight into how others perceive these phrases. It's all about finding common ground, like a dance where everyone learns the steps together.

Remember that clichés can build bridges or erect barriers when engaging with people from different backgrounds. They hold the potential to connect us through shared experiences and universal truths, yet they also require careful handling to avoid missteps. Communication is an art form, and clichés are just one brushstroke on the canvas of dialogue. So, whether you're chatting with a friend across town or the world, keep in mind that understanding goes beyond words. It's about the feelings, values, and stories hidden within them, waiting to be discovered.

Digital Dialogue: Memes and Modern Clichés

In the digital age, clichés have found new life through memes, those quirky images, and phrases that spread faster than butter on warm toast. Take "Keep Calm and Carry On," a phrase originally designed to boost morale during World War II. It's now a staple of internet culture, splashed across everything from T-shirts to coffee mugs, often with a cheeky twist. The internet has a knack for taking these classic sayings and giving them a modern makeover. Memes have become the perfect vehicle for this transformation, packaging an old idea with a fresh, funny, or sometimes absurd image that resonates with the online crowd.

Memes have turned the act of spreading clichés into an art form. The memeification of classic sayings involves more than just slapping a phrase on a funny picture; it's about capturing the zeitgeist and making it relatable to a global audience. Visual culture has amplified certain phrases, taking them from niche to ubiquitous in a few days. Remember "Doge" with its "much wow" and "such meme"? It took an ordinary dog and turned it into an internet sensation, complete with its clichés. Viral catchphrases thrive in this environment, bouncing around social media like ping-pong balls in a hurricane, reaching millions before you can say "trending." Often humorous or satirical, these phrases capture the collective mood, creating a shared language that transcends borders.

But here's the kicker: digital clichés have the lifespan of a mayfly. One day, a meme is everywhere, the next, it's as forgotten as last week's leftovers. The rapid life cycle of digital clichés means they can emerge and fade at an astonishing pace. With its ever-changing lexicon, Internet slang is the perfect example of this fleeting nature. Words and phrases like "lit," "on fleek," or "yeet" rise to prominence, only to be replaced by the next big thing. It's a linguistic revolving door, where the old is constantly being swapped out for the new. This ephemeral quality keeps the online world buzzing with fresh content, but it also means that keeping up with the latest trends can feel like chasing a runaway train.

What's particularly captivating is how these digital clichés seamlessly weave into our offline conversations, a phenomenon that underscores the pervasive influence of the internet on modern communication. Originating from the so-called "wild west" of early online chat rooms and burgeoning social media platforms, text-speak has now permeated everyday vernacular. It is not uncommon to hear someone audibly chuckle and say "LOL" instead of laughing, or to use "hashtag blessed" in verbal descriptions, merging the realms of digital shorthand with traditional spoken language. This evolution serves as a compelling testament to the Internet's formidable capability to sculpt and redefine the parameters of language, effectively eroding the distinctions between our online and offline interactions. The dynamism of this interaction has revolutionized our communicative practices, elevating digital clichés from mere online banter to significant elements of real-world discourse. As such, when "OMG" slips into your casual conversation, it's a vivid reminder of the indelible imprint the digital age has stamped on our collective lexicon, merging digital expressions with our everyday language in a manner that is both whimsical and profound.

The Role of Clichés in Persuasion and Rhetoric

Imagine a politician standing at a podium, delivering a speech to a crowd of thousands. The air is thick with anticipation, and then it happens—a phrase so familiar and well-worn that you can almost recite it in unison: "We stand at a crossroads." It's a classic move that uses clichés to tap into collective understanding. Politicians love these phrases because they're like comfort blankets for the masses. They wrap their messages in the warm familiarity of clichés, making them easy for everyone to grasp, much like a catchy chorus that sticks in your head long after the song has ended. They're strategic rhetoric tools, helping shape narratives, sway opinions, and ignite passions. Politicians can rally a crowd by relying on familiar phrases, creating a sense of unity and purpose.

But here's the rub: balance. There are too many clichés, and a speech risks sounding like a broken record. The challenge lies in crafting a message that's both memorable and original, one that resonates without resorting to a string of tired phrases. Crafting unique, yet impactful speeches requires a delicate dance between the familiar and the fresh. It's like making a classic dish with a twist—keeping the essence but adding a new flavor. The trick is to sprinkle in clichés sparingly, using them as touchstones within a broader tapestry of original thought. This approach keeps the audience engaged, offering the comfort of the known alongside the intrigue of the new. It's about finding that sweet spot where cliché and originality coexist, creating a relatable and refreshing message.

Certain clichés have become iconic in persuasive communication, consistently striking a chord with audiences. Think of "Change we can believe in"—a phrase that's as catchy as it is powerful. It embodies a promise, a vision, and a call to action, all wrapped up in a neat little package. These phrases gain traction because they encapsulate complex ideas in simple terms, resonating with listeners on both an intellectual and emotional level. They become rallying cries, mantras that inspire and motivate. It's the linguistic equivalent of a power chord in a rock anthem—simple yet incredibly effective at stirring the soul. The best clichés in rhetoric are those that capture the zeitgeist, reflecting the hopes and dreams of their time.

Yet, with great power comes great responsibility. The use of clichés in persuasion often treads a fine line between authenticity and manipulation. In advertising, for example, clichés can evoke familiarity and trust, but they can also manipulate perceptions. The intent behind the message matters as much as the words themselves. Is the cliché used to connect with the audience genuinely, or is it a tactic to gloss over more profound issues? This is where ethical considerations come into play. Audiences today are more discerning and wary of being hoodwinked by slick words and empty promises. Authenticity is key, and a cliché used without sincerity can backfire, eroding trust rather than building it. It's a reminder that while clichés can be powerful tools, they must be wielded with care and integrity.

Rhetoric is an art, and clichés are its palette—colors that, when used wisely, can paint a picture that captivates and persuades. They're the building blocks of speeches that resonate and endure, providing a foundation for new ideas. But like any tool, they require skill and discernment. The challenge lies in knowing when to use them and when to let originality take the lead. In the end, clichés remind us that while the words may be familiar, their impact depends on their intention.

Chapter 3: Clichés and Humor

Picture this: you're sitting in a comedy club, the lights dim, and the spotlight hits the stage. The comedian approaches the mic and asks, "Why did the chicken cross the road?" You can almost hear the collective eye-roll from the audience. It's a setup as old as time, but here's the kicker: it still gets laughs. Why? Because there's something inherently funny about knowing what's coming next. It's like the comfort of your favorite sitcom rerun—predictable yet satisfying. Clichés in humor tap into this psychological comfort. They create a sense of anticipation, a warm-up act for the punchline everyone knows is coming. Just as a well-worn pair of jeans fits just right, a predictable joke feels familiar and safe. You laugh not because you're surprised, but because you're in on the joke, part of the in-crowd that gets it.

The magic of humor lies in the delicate balance between predictability and surprise. Comedians are masters at setting up expectations with clichés, only to pull the rug out from under you with a twist. It's like setting up a tea party and replacing the Earl Grey with hot sauce. Take the classic setup of "Why did the chicken cross the road?" Sure, we all know the punchline, but a skilled comedian might follow with a curve-ball, like, "To binge-watch Netflix on the other side." The unexpected twist keeps the audience on their toes, their laughter a testament to the joy of being caught off guard. This balancing act is a staple of comedic genius, where the setup lulls you into a false sense of security before the punchline hits you like a cream pie to the face.

Timing is everything in comedy, and when it comes to clichés, timing is the secret sauce. A well-timed delivery can elevate a joke from a polite chuckle to a full-blown belly laugh. Think of sitcoms, where the comedic timing is as precise as a Swiss watch. The pause before the punchline, and the comedic beat that gives the audience a moment to brace themselves—are the hallmarks of great comedy. In stand-up, timing is the comedian's best friend. It's the difference between a joke landing like a feather or a lead balloon. A well-delivered cliché, perfectly timed, can be the highlight of a set, leaving the audience in stitches. As any comedian will tell you, it's not just what you say, but when you say it that counts.

Clichés aren't just for stand-up. They thrive in various comedic forms, from improv to sketches to scripted comedy. Take improv games, for instance, where clichés are the building blocks of spontaneous humor. Players might start with a cliché, like "When pigs fly," and then riff on it, creating scenes that are as unpredictable as they are hilarious. The cliché serves as a jumping-off point, a familiar platform from which creativity can soar. In sketches, clichés provide a shorthand that audiences immediately understand, allowing comedians to subvert expectations and deliver fresh laughs. Even in scripted comedy, clichés serve as signposts that guide the audience through the narrative while leaving room for comedic detours.

Exercise: Cliché Twist Challenge

The Cliché Innovation Lab dives into the art of comedic subversion by taking a well-worn cliché and flipping it on its head. Begin with a familiar phrase like "The early bird catches the worm," and then, challenge yourself to re-imagine it. What if, in your world, the early bird doesn't catch the worm but instead encounters an unexpected twist of fate? Perhaps it's the early bird who ends up in a surprising predicament, catching a cold from the dewy morning air, or maybe our proverbial worm has turned the tables, adopting the nocturnal habits of an owl and evading capture by returning home from a night out just in time. Engage with friends, family, or fellow comedians in this creative exercise, pushing each other to invent the most original and whimsical twists. This playful challenge stretches your creative capabilities and allows you to appreciate the versatility and inherent humor found within clichés when viewed through a fresh lens.

Clichés in humor serve as a bridge between the warmth of familiarity and the thrill of surprise. They function as the reliable companion to the punchlines lead role, poised to both bolster and astonish with their presence. These time-honored tropes offer a comforting handshake to the audience, setting the stage for the punchline to deliver its unexpected jolt of joy. Whether your chuckles are elicited by a joke's impeccable timing or you find yourself weaving your inventive twist into a well-known saying, clichés underscore the profound truth that laughter often resonates most deeply when it emerges from the realms of the well-trodden and the familiar.

Twisting Expectations: Clichés in Stand-Up Comedy

Stand-up comedy is a wild beast, and clichés are its tamer. Comedians wield these phrases like a magician with a deck of cards, flicking them out with the finesse of a seasoned pro. The key lies in subverting them, turning the expected into the unexpected. One technique is the misleading setup. Picture a comedian beginning with, "You know what they say, 'If at first you don't succeed…'" The audience braces for the predictable, but instead, they're hit with, "…maybe skydiving isn't for you." It's a classic bait-and-switch, where the familiar path leads to a cliffhanger of hilarity. Another favorite approach is reversing the cliché's meaning. Take the phrase, "What goes up must come down." A comedian might quip, "Unless it's your hopes and dreams—those just stay up there, taunting you." In both cases, the audience's expectations are expertly played, leaving them in stitches as they appreciate the clever twists.

Some comedians have turned this into an art form. George Carlin, the legendary wordsmith, was a maestro at twisting language and clichés. He'd dissect a phrase like "the American dream" with such precision that you'd see it from a whole new angle, often darker and more profound. Carlin's routines were a linguistic workout, challenging audiences to rethink the words they took for granted. His ability to flip clichés on their heads not only made people laugh but also made them think. Carlin's genius lay in his capacity to show the absurdity in the everyday, using clichés as his canvas and comedy as his brush.

The audience plays a crucial role in this comedic dance. They're passive observers and active participants in the joke's journey. Their awareness of clichés enhances the comedic effect, as they anticipate the familiar only to be pleasantly surprised. In comedy clubs, audience participation is the secret sauce that spices up the act. Laughter becomes a dialogue, a shared experience between the comedian and the crowd. When a comedian subverts a well-worn phrase, the audience responds with knowing laughter, acknowledging the clever twist on something they all recognize. It's a shared inside joke, a nod to the collective understanding of the cliché, and the joy of seeing it turned on its head.

There's more to twisted clichés than laughter—they can also serve as sharp social commentary. By subverting clichés, comedians often highlight societal norms, poking fun at the absurdities of modern life. Humor becomes a mirror, reflecting the quirks and contradictions of society. A comedian might take the phrase "money can't buy happiness" and twist it to comment on consumer culture, saying, "But it sure can buy countless therapy sessions." These comedic twists highlight the ridiculousness of certain societal beliefs, prompting audiences to question and reconsider what they take for granted.

Subverting clichés in comedy transcends mere humor. It's an art that engages the audience on a deeper level, challenging their preconceived notions and encouraging a more critical perspective of the world around them. Using humor as a vehicle, comedians can deliver poignant messages and insights that resonate long after the laughter subsides. As you immerse yourself in the vibrant atmosphere of a comedy show, observe the intricate dance of words and wit. Notice how comedians skillfully manipulate familiar phrases, breathing new life into them through unexpected twists and turns. These moments of brilliance often lie in the most unassuming setups, waiting to surprise and delight you with their ingenuity. This experience is not just about catching the punchlines but appreciating the craftsmanship behind them, revealing the cleverness that thrives within the realm of the expected, and leaving you with a profound appreciation for the power of language and laughter.

Creating Punchlines: Innovative Uses of Old Sayings

Consider clichés as the old shoes of language—comfortable, and reliable, but sometimes in need of a good polish to make them sparkle anew. Crafting fresh punchlines from tired phrases is like giving those shoes a snazzy new shine. Start by gathering a group of comedians or friends for a brainstorming session. Toss around common sayings and see who can create the most outrageous twists. The goal is to break the mold, to take the familiar and push it into the realm of the unexpected. Picture this: "When life gives you lemons..." Sure, you could make lemonade, but how about "making a lemon meringue pie and charging five bucks a slice"? Suddenly, the cliché is transformed, morphing into something fresh and funny.

Wordplay is the ace up your sleeve during this linguistic transformation journey. Puns, in particular, are a powerful tool to inject vigor into time-worn expressions. Imagine the classic pun, "Two peanuts walk into a bar..." This setup thrives on wordplay, morphing a straightforward phrase into a punchline with an unexpectedly whimsical twist. The essence of wordplay lies in exploiting the multifaceted meanings and auditory nuances of words, thereby concocting humor from the peculiarities inherent in language itself. The objective is to navigate to that elusive juncture where language dances with playfulness, and a strategically deployed pun transforms a cliché teetering on the edge of eye-roll territory into a moment bursting with laughter. The artistry involves maintaining a delicate balance, ensuring the wordplay amplifies the comedic value without detracting from the essence of the humor.

Comedy thrives on observation, and some of the best routines come from re-imagining clichés through the lens of everyday life. Take Ellen DeGeneres, who often employs observational humor to great effect. She takes the mundane and spins it into comedy gold. Focusing on the details, she finds the absurdity in the ordinary, using clichés as a springboard for her unique perspective. This approach allows her to connect with her audience personally, as they see their lives reflected in her routines. It's a reminder that sometimes the best humor is rooted in the familiar, seen through fresh eyes. Observational humor leverages the cliché's relatability while injecting it with originality.

Culture plays a significant role in how we interpret humor, especially when it comes to clichés. What's funny in one culture might fall flat in another, so understanding cultural context is key. A joke that relies on a specific cultural reference might resonate deeply with one audience but leave another scratching their heads. This is why some comedians succeed internationally—they tap into universal truths while respecting local nuances. Humor is a powerful tool for breaking down barriers but requires a deft touch to navigate different cultural landscapes. A well-crafted punchline considers these nuances, ensuring the humor lands as intended.

Clichés may be old hat, but they offer endless possibilities for creative reinvention. They're the foundation upon which new jokes can be built, a starting point for exploration rather than a final destination. The next time you reach for a well-worn phrase, challenge yourself to flip it on its head. Look for the humor hidden in plain sight; don't be afraid to take risks. After all, comedy is about pushing boundaries, discovering joy in unforeseen circumstances, and transforming the mundane into the remarkable.

Humor Across Cultures: Clichés as a Universal Language

Humor, much like a good cup of coffee, knows no bounds. It crosses oceans and climbs mountains, uniting people under the banner of laughter. At the heart of this global giggle-fest lies the humble cliché, a linguistic chameleon that adapts to different tongues and cultures. In comedy, clichés act as universal touchstones, tickling funny bones from Tokyo to Timbuktu. Common comedic themes, such as slapstick or the classic battle of the sexes, find their bread and butter in clichés. They're the comedic glue that binds us, allowing a joke about in-laws or lazy teenagers to resonate, whether delivered in Swahili or Swedish. Even when cultural nuances shift, the core humor of clichés holds strong, a testament to their timeless appeal.

But translating humor? That's a different ball game. Imagine trying to explain the pun "olive you" to someone whose language has no equivalent for "olive" and "I love." Some jokes don't make the trip across borders. They get lost in translation, like a tourist without a map. This is particularly true for clichés, where the humor often hinges on language-specific quirks. The French might chuckle at "C'est la vie," but a direct translation to "That's life" might not carry the same je ne sais quoi. The humor that thrives in one language can wilt in another, much like a soufflé that collapses when faced with a different oven.

Every culture has its clichés that tickle the funny bone in unique ways. Take the expression "the elephant in the room." In English, it's a metaphor for an obvious problem no one wants to acknowledge. However, in other cultures, the idiom might involve different animals or objects. In Japanese, there's the phrase "にらず" (fukusui bon ni kaerazu), meaning "spilled water will not return to the tray," which humorously highlights irreversible mistakes. Local idioms add spice to the comedic mix, providing a glimpse into cultural values and humor styles. They're like secret passwords that unlock laughter within their cultural context, offering comedic value that's both specific and enlightening.

In today's interconnected world, the potential for cross-cultural comedic collaborations is greater than ever. Imagine a French comedian teaming up with a Brazilian one, each bringing their cultural clichés to the table, blending them into a comedic gumbo that's rich and varied. International comedy festivals serve as melting pots, where humor transcends language barriers, and clichés become shared experiences. These festivals are fertile ground for comedians to experiment, to riff on clichés that might be universal or uniquely cultural, creating comedy that speaks to the human condition in all its glorious diversity.

Such collaborations encourage comedians to step out of their cultural comfort zones and embrace the shared language of laughter. They highlight the universality of certain themes while celebrating the peculiarities of different comedic traditions. Humor becomes a bridge, connecting disparate cultures through the shared joy of a well-timed joke. It's a reminder that while words might differ, the laughter they inspire is a universal constant, echoing across borders and bringing people together in a way that few other expressions can.

Overcoming Audience Fatigue: Avoiding Stale Jokes

Few scenarios are as lethal to the vibrancy of a comedy performance as encountering an audience that has mentally exited the venue. Picture the scene: a dimly lit comedy club filled with patrons whose arms are tightly folded, their expressions blank, as the person on stage recycles the same tired, "been there, done that" lines. The air is heavy with a collective sense of ennui, a palpable yawn threatening to engulf the room. This type of audience disengagement acts like a contagion, spreading rapidly through the crowd if the material fails to resonate. To identify when your comedic routine is in dire need of rejuvenation, observe the audience's reactions closely: tepid applause, half-hearted chuckles, or, in the most dire situations, an oppressive silence. These indicators serve as glaring red flags, signaling that it's time to administer some much-needed CPR—Comedy Performance Resuscitation— to breathe life back into your act.

So, how do comedians breathe new life into old jokes? It starts with a little creative elbow grease. Rewriting exercises can do wonders. Take a tired joke, strip it to its bare bones, and rebuild it with fresh material. Add a dash of wit, a sprinkle of current events, and voila! You've got something that feels as fresh as a morning breeze. Incorporating topical references can make the material feel relevant and timely, like weaving a news headline into your punchline. It keeps the audience on their toes, wondering what you'll tackle next, and ensures your act doesn't feel stuck in a time warp.

Originality is comedy's lifeblood, and it keeps audiences coming back for more. There's a thrill in hearing a perspective that hasn't been done to death. Originality workshops can be a goldmine for comedians looking to hone their craft. Picture a room full of comedians, bouncing ideas off each other like a game of creative ping-pong. It's a chance to break out of the cliché cycle, explore uncharted comedic territory, and push the boundaries of what's expected. The goal is to find your unique voice, something special that sets you apart from the crowd. Whether it's an unexpected twist on a mundane topic or a fresh take on an old trope, originality is the key to keeping your material vibrant.

Audience feedback is a comedian's best friend. It's the mirror that reflects the true impact of your jokes. Open mic nights are the perfect testing grounds, where comedians can throw their material against the wall and see what sticks. It's like a comedy lab, where trial and error reign supreme. Listen to the audience, gauge their reactions, and refine your jokes accordingly. Sometimes, the best ideas come from the most unexpected places—a chuckle from the back of the room or a suggestion from a fellow comedian. Embrace the feedback, even when it stings, and use it to sharpen your comedic edge.

Remember, comedy is a living, breathing art form. It's not static; it evolves with each performance, each audience, and each joke. Avoiding stale material requires a commitment to growth, to constantly challenging yourself to be better, funnier, and more innovative. It's about staying one step ahead of audience fatigue, ensuring that your act remains as dynamic and engaging as the first time you took the stage.

From Script to Stage: Practical Exercises for Comedians

Creating comedic gold from clichés requires more than just a clever twist of words; it involves honing your craft through practice, experimentation, and spontaneity. One practical exercise to kick-start creativity is free writing. Grab a pen, set a timer, and let your thoughts flow without judgment. Pick a cliché like "all's well that ends well," and let your mind wander. Write down anything that comes to mind, no matter how absurd. This exercise is like shaking the cobwebs out of your brain, freeing up space for originality. You might find yourself stumbling upon a nugget of humor that turns a tired phrase into a punchline as fresh as morning dew.

Once you've got some material, it's time to play with delivery. How a joke is delivered can make or break it, so experimenting with different styles is worth experimenting. Try some role-playing exercises where you perform the same joke in multiple ways: deadpan, over-the-top, or with a dramatic flair. This practice helps you discover which delivery style resonates best with your material and audience. It's also a great way to break out of your comfort zone and explore new comedic personas. Maybe you'll find that a joke about traffic jams works best when delivered with the exasperation of someone who's perpetually late.

Rehearsals are the unsung heroes of comedy. Practicing your material is like fine-tuning an instrument. It sharpens your comedic timing and lets you iron out any wrinkles before you hit the stage. Record your performances and watch them back, taking note of where the laughs land and where the silence stretches a bit too long. This feedback loop is invaluable, providing insights into how your material is received and where it could use a little polish. It's like having a personal comedy coach who's brutally honest but always rooting for your success.

Engaging with diverse audiences is an art in itself. Not every joke will hit the same way with different crowds, so tailoring your humor is crucial. Audience profiling can be a helpful tool here. Consider the demographics of your audience and what might resonate with them. A joke about internet memes might fly over the heads of a more mature crowd but will have teenagers in stitches. On the flip side, a witty observation about the pitfalls of homeownership might unite a room full of adults. Understanding your audience ensures that your humor lands where it's supposed to, making your act relatable and impactful.

Improvisation keeps your material fresh and your mind sharp. Improv exercises are like mental gymnastics, training you to think on your feet and adapt to whatever the comedy gods throw your way. Practice quick-thinking drills where you respond to random prompts or pick a cliché and riff on it spontaneously. This keeps your performances lively and prevents your act from becoming stale. Improv also builds confidence, teaching you to trust your instincts and embrace the unexpected. It's the comedic equivalent of jazz, where the magic happens at the moment, and every performance is a unique experience.

In the grand comedy theater, clichés are both the script and the improvisation. They're the familiar notes you play and the unexpected solos that surprise and delight. As you refine your craft, remember that humor is a living, breathing entity, constantly evolving with each performance and each audience. Whether crafting new jokes, experimenting with delivery, or embracing the spontaneity of improv, the stage is your playground, and laughter is the ultimate reward.

Chapter 4: Clichés in Writing and Literature

Writing is like baking a cake; sometimes you nail it, and sometimes you end up with a crooked mess of frosting and crumbs. And just like baking, writing has its fair share of pitfalls. Enter clichés, those pesky little expressions that sneak into your prose like uninvited guests at a wedding. They're the linguistic equivalent of selfies—everywhere, and not always welcome. But why do these old chestnuts often go unnoticed by writers themselves? It's the writer's dilemma: spotting clichés in your work is like trying to see the back of your head. You know they're lurking, but they're surprisingly difficult to pinpoint.

Whether seasoned or just starting, writers often fall into the trap of clichés because they're familiar sounds. Like a comforting tune playing softly in the background, they offer a sense of ease, filling the gaps when words fail to come. But this familiarity can become a blind spot, rendering you oblivious to their overuse. It's like having a mustard stain on your shirt that everyone notices except you. To combat this, self-assessment techniques become crucial. Take a step back from your writing, read it with fresh eyes, and hunt for those repeated phrases that seem to echo like a broken record. Better yet, enlist a peer review. Fellow writers can be like those brutally honest friends who tell you when you've got spinach in your teeth. They'll spot clichés you've glossed over, helping you polish your prose to a gleaming shine.

When identifying clichés in drafts, think of it as a treasure hunt, but instead of gold, you're searching for stale expressions. Highlight any phrases that seem all too familiar. If you arm yourself with a red pen and meticulously comb through your latest draft, circling every cliché that rears its familiar head. Challenge yourself to reinvent these worn-out phrases with inventive, original expressions that breathe new life into your narrative. This rigorous exercise serves a dual purpose: it sharpens your ability to detect clichés with laser precision and fosters a culture of creative innovation within your writing process. Once you've reworked your draft into a fresher version of its former self, initiate a peer review session. Present your rejuvenated manuscript to a trusted colleague or friend, inviting them to critique the newly minted phrases. This collaborative exchange often illuminates the effectiveness of your revisions, revealing how your prose has evolved to captivate and resonate more deeply with readers. The insidious nature of clichés, acting as creativity's most cunning adversaries, has the power to dull the sparkle of even the most vivid narratives, rendering them mundane. Acknowledging the pervasive influence of clichés on your writing marks a pivotal first stride in the journey to transcend them. By nurturing an aptitude for recognizing and innovatively replacing clichés, you embark on a trans-formative process. This evolution refines your writing from a tapestry of predictability to a dynamic showcase of originality, guaranteeing to engage the curiosity and ignite the imagination of your audience with every turn of the page. *"In the nick of time"* or *"head over heels"* More than once, it's time for a rewrite. Analyze your sentence structures for predictability. If your story unfolds like a worn-out road map, it might be time to detour and explore new routes. Consider the genres you're writing in. Romance novels often fall into the "love at first sight" trap, while fantasy tales can't seem to resist the allure of "the chosen one." These clichés can be like that piece of broccoli in your teeth—challenging to spot but glaringly obvious to others.

Clichés can significantly hinder reader engagement, much like a poor Wi-Fi connection—frustrating and likely to cause exasperation. They can reduce a reader's interest more quickly than the phrase, "Been there, done that." Predictable plots, filled with clichés, lead to reader fatigue, making the narrative feel as if it is on autopilot. Readers desire originality and are more inclined to invest in a story that provides fresh perspectives and unexpected twists, rather than one that recycles familiar tropes. To maintain your audience's interest, challenge yourself to replace clichés with unique expressions that stimulate curiosity and evoke emotion. By understanding the nuances of emotional expression, as explored in *The Art of Emotions: Your Brain on Feelings*, writers can avoid stale language and craft more impactful narratives. This deeper understanding of how emotions work, as detailed in this book, allows for richer character development and more authentic storytelling.

Exercise: Cliché Cleanse

Embark on a meticulous quest with a red pen in hand, meticulously identifying every cliché that dots the landscape of your latest draft. Each identified cliché presents an opportunity to infuse creativity; replace it with an innovative, original phrase that adds zest to your narrative. This rigorous exercise sharpens your vigilance against clichés and fosters an environment where creative expression thrives. After revitalizing your manuscript with fresh verbiage, initiate a collaborative critique by sharing your work with a confidante. Solicit their insights on your novel expressions. This exchange often unveils the newfound vibrancy and engagement of your prose, a testament to your involvement as a writer.

The insidious nature of clichés, those cunning adversaries of creativity, can stealthily transform a once-vivid narrative into a mundane recount. Recognizing their pervasive influence in your prose is crucial, marking a significant stride towards their mastery. By cultivating an acute awareness and actively seeking inventive replacements, you embark on a transformative journey. This evolution not only polishes your writing into a dynamic showcase of originality but also ensures it captivates the curiosity and fuels the imagination of your audience, turning each page into a discovery instead of a predictable procession.

Crafting New Expressions: Exercises for Originality

Writing is like cooking; you need the ingredients to create something delicious. But sometimes, you find yourself stuck with the same old recipe, and it's time to spice things up. Enter creative exercises, the secret sauce to whisk your writing from bland to brilliant. One of the best ways to kick-start creativity is through free writing. Grab a pen and paper, set a ten-minute timer, and write without stopping. Don't worry about grammar or punctuation—just let your thoughts flow like a river after a storm. This exercise helps you dig deep into your subconscious and uncover original ideas that might have been lurking beneath the surface, waiting to be discovered like hidden treasures.

Another playful exercise is "word association" games. Start with a random word—"apple"—and jot down the first thing that comes to mind. Perhaps you think of "pie," which leads you to "grandma's kitchen," and suddenly, you're reminiscing about childhood summers. These associations can lead to fresh expressions and novel ideas, taking your writing in unexpected directions. It's like a mental game of hopscotch, where each leap brings you closer to a new combination of words that can replace the tired clichés you've been using. These games are not just fun; they're a workout for your brain, flexing your creative muscles and helping you build a repertoire of unique phrases.

Re-imagining common phrases is another way to break free from the cliché shackles. Take a cliché you've used a thousand times and rewrite it with a personal twist. For example, instead of "biting the bullet," try "sipping the storm" to convey facing challenges calmly. This approach makes your writing feel more authentic, drawing from your own experiences and emotions. You can also turn clichés into questions to explore them further. Instead of saying "the elephant in the room," ask yourself, "What's the uninvited guest at this party?" This method uncovers new expressions and deepens your engagement with the subject, making your writing more thoughtful and engaging.

Sensory details can transform your writing from black-and-white to Technicolor, replacing generic phrases with vivid imagery. Think of how a scene comes alive when you describe the *"crisp, golden leaves crunching underfoot on a brisk autumn day"* rather than just saying *"It was fall."* Engage all five senses in your prose to create a rich tapestry of experiences for your readers. Let them taste the tartness of a lemon, feel the sun's warmth on their skin, and hear the distant call of a seagull. Visual imagery in descriptive writing evokes emotions and memories, drawing readers into your world and making them feel part of the story.

Examples of cliché transformations abound in literature, where writers have taken familiar phrases and given them a new lease on life. Consider how "bite the bullet" morphs into "sip the storm," a metaphor that suggests facing adversity with grace. Or how "a needle in a haystack" becomes "finding a whisper in a hurricane," offering a fresh take on the idea of something elusive. These transformations aren't just clever; they're invitations to see the world through a different lens, challenging readers to reconsider how they perceive familiar concepts. The beauty of these new expressions lies in their ability to surprise and delight, turning the ordinary into something extraordinary.

So, grab your creative toolkit and start crafting expressions that dance off the page. With a little practice and a lot of imagination, you'll find that the possibilities are as endless as your curiosity.

The Art of Metaphor: Beyond the Cliché

Imagine you're at a party—everyone's milling about, making small talk. Then someone throws out a zinger or a metaphor—something so vivid it paints a picture in your mind. Suddenly, you're not just hearing words but seeing, feeling, maybe even tasting them. That's the magic of a well-crafted metaphor. It's like a splash of color in an otherwise monochrome world. Metaphors have the power to enrich language, adding layers of depth and originality that mere descriptions can't quite capture. They transform an ordinary idea, turning a simple sentence into a feast for the imagination. Crafting these gems involves comparison techniques that allow two seemingly unrelated things to come together in a harmonious dance of words. It's about finding that sweet spot where a metaphor fits and elevates your narrative.

Creating original metaphors is like embarking on a treasure hunt. Inspiration is scattered around us, hiding in plain sight within nature and the everyday. Picture this: the sun dips below the horizon, not just setting, but "spilling a pot of molten gold across the sky." Or consider the mundane chore of washing dishes, transformed into "a tiny war waged against the tyranny of grease." By drawing from the world around us, we can craft fresh, impactful, and evocative metaphors. They breathe life into writing, like adding spices to a dish, transforming it from bland to unforgettable. The key is observing keenly, letting nature and daily life guide your creative process.

Authors like Toni Morrison have wielded metaphors with the precision of a master painter, using them to convey complex ideas and emotions gracefully. Morrison employs metaphorical language in her novels to explore themes of identity, history, and trauma. Her metaphors aren't just decorative; they serve as bridges, connecting readers to the deeper truths within her narratives. Contemporary poetry, too, thrives on the power of metaphor, using it to distill vast emotions into a few potent lines. Poets play with language, bending it to their will, crafting metaphors that resonate and linger like a haunting melody. These literary works demonstrate the power of metaphor to transform the mundane into the extraordinary, elevating the art of storytelling to new heights.

Yet, while metaphors can enrich and enliven writing, they also walk a fine line between clarity and confusion. A metaphor should illuminate, not obscure, the meaning behind the words. This balance is crucial. Imagine navigating a dense jungle of mixed metaphors, each vying for attention, resulting in a tangled mess that frustrates readers. Avoiding mixed metaphors is as important as the metaphor itself; unity is key. A single, well-chosen metaphor can do more than a dozen jumbled ones. It acts as a guiding star, lighting the way for readers and ensuring that the narrative remains clear and compelling.

The art of metaphor lies in its ability to transform language, offering a fresh perspective and inviting readers to see the world in new ways. Like a prism refracting light, a metaphor can reveal hidden facets of a concept, enhancing understanding and engagement. As you explore the limitless possibilities of metaphor, remember that it's not about using them for the sake of it, but about choosing the right one to enrich your story. The best metaphors feel inevitable as if they were always meant to be part of the narrative. They leave an indelible mark, making your writing memorable and alive.

Inspiring Creativity: Embracing Unique Storytelling

Ever feel like your story is on a straight path, like a train on tracks, chugging predictably from start to finish? Time to shake things up. Experimenting with narrative structure is like giving your story a good caffeine jolt. Non-linear timelines can add a dash of intrigue, taking your readers on a wild ride through time. Think of it as the literary equivalent of a Christopher Nolan film—start at the end, hop to the middle, and then reveal the beginning.

This approach keeps readers on their toes, piecing the puzzle together. Or, consider using multiple points of view. Let each character have their say, like a group chat where everyone's got a juicy story to spill. This adds depth and dimension, offering readers a panoramic view of your world and its inhabitants.

Voice and style are your signature, the unique flair that makes your writing memorable. Crafting distinct narrative voices is like casting different actors in a play, each bringing their quirks and nuances to the stage. Experiment with tone and style the way a chef might play with spices—bold here, subtle there. Maybe try a dry, sarcastic voice for one character and a lyrical, poetic style for another. Doing this creates a mosaic of perspectives, each piece contributing to the overall picture. Your voice should resonate like a catchy tune, one that readers can't help but hum along to. It's not just about what you say, but how you say it that sets your work apart.

Finding inspiration can sometimes feel like hunting for a needle in a haystack, but the trick is to look beyond the obvious. Draw from personal experiences and dreams, those quirky, surreal snippets that play out in your mind while you sleep. They're often rich with emotion and unique imagery, perfect for weaving into your narratives. Life itself is full of strange and wonderful moments waiting to be captured. Observe the world with a writer's eye, noticing the little details others might miss—the way rain dances on a windowpane, or the symphony of sounds in a bustling café. These observations can spark ideas, turning the mundane into the magical. It's about seeing the world as both participant and spectator, where every moment is a potential story waiting to unfold.

Incorporating diverse cultural perspectives into your storytelling is like adding new colors to your palette. Blend folklore from various cultures, mixing myths and legends with modern tales to create something fresh and exciting. Multicultural characters and settings enrich your narratives, offering readers a glimpse into worlds they might not have encountered. This adds depth to your stories and reflects the diverse tapestry of the real world. Celebrating different voices and experiences is a chance to make your work resonate with a wider audience. Whether it's the mystical tales of the East or the vibrant folklore of Latin America, these stories provide a treasure trove of inspiration, waiting to be explored and brought to life in new and unexpected ways.

Experimentation stands as the pulsating core of creative endeavors, the catalyst that propels narratives beyond the mundane and into the realm of the extraordinary. It is the act of venturing into uncharted territories, of daring to defy the conventional and embrace the novel. Whether you're weaving a tale through a labyrinth of non-linear timelines, giving life to a chorus of divergent voices, or infusing your narrative with the rich hues of diverse cultural landscapes, the objective remains constant: to imbue your storytelling with a dynamism and vibrancy that mirrors the kaleidoscopic complexity of the world we inhabit. This pursuit of innovation is not merely an exercise in stylistic flair but a commitment to crafting stories that resonate with authenticity and depth. By challenging the boundaries of traditional storytelling, you invite your readers to journey with you into realms brimming with possibility, where each page turned is an invitation to explore the boundless potential of the human imagination.

Editing with Precision: Cliché Spotting Techniques

Editing your work is like trying to cut your hair: tricky, and often resulting in a lot of head-scratching. But fear not, fellow wordsmiths, for there are ways to trim those pesky clichés from your prose without losing your sanity. First up, create a checklist of common clichés. Think of it as your linguistic hit list. You know the ones: *"better late than never," "think outside the box,"* and their cronies. Keep this list handy as you comb through your drafts, rooting out these tired phrases like weeds in a garden. And if your eyes start to glaze over from staring at your own words too long, consider enlisting the help of software tools designed to detect overused phrases. These digital bloodhounds can sniff out clichés faster than you can say "quick as a flash."

Of course, even the most diligent writer can become blind to their work. It's like trying to see the forest for the trees when you're smack-dab in the middle of it. That's why taking a step back is crucial. Put your draft away for a few days, let it marinate, and then return with fresh eyes. The distance will help you spot those sneaky clichés hiding in plain sight. Another trick is reading your work aloud. It's remarkable how different your words sound when they're out in the open air, rather than stuck inside your head. Those repetitive phrases that seemed so clever on paper might suddenly sound like a broken record. Plus, your cat will love hearing your story.

Precision in language is like seasoning in cooking: too little, and the dish is bland; too much, and you can't taste anything else. To refine your language, focus on word choice. Conduct exercises that challenge you to choose words with precision and clarity. Swap out "walked" for "sauntered" or "rushed" depending on the mood you want to convey. It's all about finding that perfect word that captures exactly what you're trying to say without leaning on clichés. The right word can sing a sentence, while the wrong one can leave it flat. It's like assembling a jigsaw puzzle—each piece must fit just right for the picture to come together.

The benefits of a rigorous editing process are like the difference between a rough sketch and a finished masterpiece. Just ask any author, who's known for their meticulous revisions. Take Hemingway, for instance. Legend has it he revised "The Old Man and the Sea" over 200 times before it was published. This relentless editing resulted in a story that flows like a river—clear, purposeful, and clutter-free. Thorough editing can elevate your writing from good to great, ensuring that your voice shines through without the noise of overused expressions. It's about polishing your prose until it gleams, making your story readable and unforgettable.

Clichés, much like the unwelcome lint clinging to a cherished sweater, can mar the fabric of your prose, rendering it dull and predictable. However, with precise and mindful editing, you have the power to eradicate these blemishes, revitalizing your writing to stand out as sharp, invigorating, and uniquely reflective of your voice. Embark on this meticulous journey with a red pen in hand, embodying the spirit of a discerning editor. As you meticulously comb through your draft, visualize yourself as an artisan, carefully chiseling away at the superfluous, until what remains is a work of art that resonates with clarity and originality. Transform your draft from a rough outline into a polished gem that captivates and endures.

Writing for Impact: Making Every Word Count

Imagine you're packing for a trip. You can't take everything, so you have to choose wisely. Writing is a bit like that. Every word should count, and sometimes that means cutting the fluff. Concise writing is about eliminating unnecessary words to strengthen your narrative. Think of it as a literary diet—trimming the excess to reveal the lean, powerful prose beneath. This doesn't mean your writing has to be dry or dull. The opposite is true. By shedding the dead weight, your words gain impact, resonating more deeply with your readers. Techniques for trimming prose can include removing redundant adjectives, avoiding repetitious descriptions, and cutting any extraneous details that don't serve the story. It's like pruning a tree; the more you remove what's unnecessary, the more vibrant and healthy the tree becomes.

Crafting impactful sentences involves a delicate dance with language. Varying sentence length is one way to create a rhythm that keeps readers engaged. Short sentences can punch through a scene, delivering a quick jab of information. Long sentences, by contrast, can draw readers into a moment, letting them linger over a thought or description. It's like orchestrating a symphony, where each note contributes to the overall harmony. Another strategy is using the active voice to bring directness and clarity to your writing. Active voice propels the narrative forward, making it feel alive and immediate. Compare "The book was read by the girl" to "The girl read the book." The latter is more engaging, pulling the reader into the action with simplicity and energy.

Strong openings and endings are the bookends of your narrative. They hold everything in place, ensuring nothing falls from your reader's memory. A memorable first line can hook readers faster than you can say "once upon a time." Consider the opening line of George Orwell's "1984": "It was a bright, cold day in April, and the clocks were striking thirteen." Immediately, you're drawn into a world that's familiar yet unsettling. Crafting these lines requires a keen sense of what will intrigue and entice your audience. At the other end, a satisfying conclusion leaves a lasting impression. It's the final note of your symphony, which lingers in the air long after the music has stopped. Techniques for achieving this can include tying up loose ends, delivering a twist, or leaving readers with a thought-provoking question.

Some authors have mastered the art of clarity and impact, and there's much to learn from their examples. Ernest Hemingway, for instance, is renowned for his economical style. His prose is like a fine-tuned machine, every part working in perfect harmony with the others. In "The Old Man and the Sea," Hemingway strips away the superfluous, leaving behind a narrative as lean as it is powerful. His short and punchy sentences drive the story forward with relentless momentum. On the other hand, Virginia Woolf's writing is a dance of lyrical sentences that weave together emotion and thought. In "Mrs. Dalloway," her prose flows like a river, carrying readers on its current. Woolf's ability to blend the internal and external worlds creates a narrative that resonates with depth and meaning, showing that power in writing comes from both what is said and how it is expressed.

As we close this chapter on writing for impact, remember that each word is a building block. Whether constructing a skyscraper of ideas or a humble cottage of thoughts, your choice of words will determine the strength and beauty of your creation. Now, let's explore how clichés can be reimagined in the digital age.

Chapter 5: Clichés in the Digital Age

Picture this: you're scrolling through your social media feed, dodging ads for socks you swear you never Googled, when you spot a post that's "gone viral." Suddenly, everyone and their grandma is talking about it, sharing it, and even their cats are tweeting about it. Welcome to the digital age, where clichés get a turbo boost thanks to the internet. "Going viral" is more than just a term for catching a nasty flu—it's a digital phenomenon where phrases spread like wildfire. Social media has turned phrases like "you only live once" or "living my best life" into viral sensations, much like that video of the roller-skating squirrel. But what makes these phrases travel faster than a clickbait headline?

Social media platforms like Twitter and Instagram are the playgrounds where clichés flourish. Algorithms, those mysterious formulas that decide what we see and when we see it, play a huge role. They're like digital matchmakers, pairing users with content that'll keep them scrolling for hours. Hashtags amplify these phrases, turning them into trending topics that everyone wants in on. If you slap a hashtag on a phrase, like #YOLO or #FOMO, it's suddenly everywhere, from your cousin's Facebook page to the Instagram Story of that kid you sat next to in third grade. These algorithms know what makes us tick—or rather, click.

Take the phrase "YOLO" for example. It burst onto the scene, became everyone's excuse for skydiving, and vanished quicker than you can say "planking." The life-cycle of a viral cliché is like a pop star's career: meteoric rise, oversaturation, then a quiet retreat into nostalgia. These phrases often ride the wave of cultural relevance, peaking when they capture the collective mood. But like any good party, they eventually wind down once everyone's had their fill. Remember when everyone was convinced that "YOLO" justified that extra shot of tequila? Now it's more of a relic, trotted out occasionally for a chuckle.

The impact of viral clichés on communication is a mixed bag. They shape our online discourse, influencing how we interact, talk, and think. Digital culture absorbs these phrases, turning them into cultural markers that define the zeitgeist. They're like linguistic snapshots of a moment, capturing the essence of a collective experience. But they also have a flip side. They can stifle originality as they saturate our feeds, reducing complex ideas to bite-sized soundbites. You might find yourself using "YOLO" instead of a more nuanced reflection on why you decided to take that impromptu road trip.

Viral clichés influence our behavior, nudging us towards certain trends and mindsets. They become part of the digital lexicon, shaping how we express ourselves online. A phrase that starts as a clever quip can quickly become a meme, a catchphrase, and eventually, a part of our everyday speech. This process democratizes language change, allowing anyone with an internet connection to contribute to the evolution of communication styles. As these clichés become embedded in digital culture, they challenge traditional linguistic theories, prompting researchers to expand their understanding of how language evolves in the digital age. It's like watching a new dialect form in real-time, complete with its rules and quirks.

Reflection Exercise: Viral Vocabulary

Contemplate a viral phrase that has woven itself into your daily lexicon. Ponder on the elements that made this phrase click with your personal or cultural context, giving it a spot in your repertoire of expressions. Delve into its journey - how did it transition from a mere string of words to a significant part of your vernacular? Assess the impact it has on the way you communicate, both in the digital realm and in face-to-face interactions. Visualize your conversations stripped of this phrase; would they retain their vibrancy, or would there be a noticeable void where its digital zest once was? This exercise is not only about recognizing the omnipresence of such phrases in our lives but also understanding their role in crafting the nuances of our communication tapestry in this digitally interconnected world.

In the relentless swirl of today's digital landscape, clichés evolve beyond simple expressions to form the very heartbeat of online communication. They serve as a swift, communal dialect for interaction, contemplation, and even compassion. As you traverse the vast expanse of your digital feed, take a moment to acknowledge the presence of these viral clichés. They act as reflective surfaces, mirroring the shifting paradigm of language while highlighting the profound impact of words in this digital epoch. Through their ubiquity, these phrases encapsulate the collective mindset, offering a lens through which we view the world and connect with others across the digital divide.

Hashtags and Headlines: The New Age of Clichés

Imagine you're snapping a selfie, ready to post it online. You sprinkle it with a few hashtags like digital confetti. Welcome to the world where hashtags are the new clichés, encapsulating complex ideas in a single word or phrase. Take #Throwback Thursday, for example. It's a nostalgic nod to the past, a digital time machine that lets you relive memories one post at a time. Then there's #Blessed, a hashtag that's less about divine intervention and more about a humblebrag. It's the social media equivalent of saying, "Look at my fabulous life!" These hashtags act like tiny billboards, broadcasting emotions, themes, and ideas in a way that words alone can't capture. They're the shorthand of the internet, turning a simple post into a statement.

Headlines, too, have become a breeding ground for clichés, especially in the clickbait era. "You won't believe what happens next!" is the digital siren call, luring you into a rabbit hole of sensationalism. These headlines are designed to grab attention like a toddler throws a tantrum—loudly and without shame. They thrive on clichés, twisting familiar phrases into irresistible promises of shock and awe. It's like the carnival barker of the internet, shouting, "Step right up and see the amazing content!" You know you're being played, but curiosity gets the better of you. It's a game of cat and mouse, where the headline is the cheese, and you're the unsuspecting rodent.

Hashtags are more than just digital decoration. They've become powerful tools in campaigns, both social and commercial. Take #MeToo, a hashtag that sparked a global movement, amplifying voices and driving change. It showed how a simple phrase could unite people, turning a hashtag into a rallying cry. Brands, too, have jumped on the hashtag bandwagon, using them to boost campaigns and engage with audiences. Trending hashtags like #BlackFridaySales or #NewYearNewMe are marketing gold, drawing in customers like moths to a flame. But there's a catch: the more a hashtag is used, the less impact it has. It's like a catchy pop song that eventually becomes background noise. Overused hashtags suffer from engagement fatigue, drowning in the digital clutter they once dominated.

So, what happens when hashtags become as common as cat videos? They lose their luster. The more a hashtag is used, the more it resembles a worn-out cliché. It's the digital equivalent of hearing "Have a nice day!"—nice, but devoid of meaning. This saturation leads to diminishing returns, diluting the initial impact over time. Users become desensitized, scrolling past hashtags as if they were white noise. It's a reminder that in the fast-paced world of social media, staying fresh and relevant is a constant challenge. Just as you wouldn't wear the same outfit to every party, you can't rely on the same hashtags to keep people engaged.

In this digital age, hashtags and headlines have become the new clichés, shaping how we communicate and interact online. They encapsulate ideas, drive engagement, and sometimes, just sometimes, change the world. But like any cliché, they walk a fine line between being powerful tools and tired tropes. So next time you're about to hashtag your latest post, remember the power—and the pitfalls—of these modern-day clichés. Keep them fresh, and relevant, and whatever you do, don't let them become the digital equivalent of yesterday's news.

Meme Culture: Humor and Clichés Redefined

Imagine the internet as a vast, bustling bazaar where memes are the hawkers of humor, peddling their wares to anyone with a Wi-Fi connection. Memes have taken the humble cliché and turned it into comedic gold, breathing new life into tired phrases with a wit as sharp as unexpected. Take the "Distracted Boyfriend" meme, for instance. It's a classic example of cliché subversion, where the familiar setup of a wandering eye and a scorned lover is turned on its head to comment on everything from consumerism to procrastination. This meme doesn't just illustrate a point; it tells a story with layers of meaning wrapped up in a single, relatable image.

The life-cycle of meme-driven clichés is as unpredictable as a cat on a hot tin roof. Memes like "Doge" and "Pepe the Frog" have gone through phases of popularity, decline, and sometimes even resurgence. "Doge," with its iconic "much wow" and "very amaze" captions, captured the Internet's heart with its endearing simplicity, only to fade as new trends emerged. Meanwhile, "Pepe the Frog" navigated a more tumultuous journey, from a harmless comic character to a symbol of controversy and back to a meme of nostalgia. Each meme has its trajectory, influenced by the ever-shifting tides of online trends and the whims of internet users.

Memes aren't just about laughs; they're a form of digital storytelling that conveys narratives through clichés. Consider the "Expanding Brain" meme. It's a visual journey through increasing levels of enlightenment, using clichés to depict everything from personal growth to absurd humor. This meme takes the cliché of enlightenment and turns it into a flexible narrative tool, allowing creators to comment on a range of topics with a simple, scalable format. The "Expanding Brain" meme doesn't just tell a story; it invites viewers to engage with the layers of meaning behind each stage, making it a dynamic and interactive expression.

What's fascinating is how memes cross cultural boundaries, becoming global phenomena with local adaptations. A meme born in the United States can find new life in Japan, reimagined with local references and humor. This global spread is a testament to memes' universal appeal and ability to transcend language barriers. They become cultural chameleons, adapting to their surroundings while retaining their core humor. Memes like "Distracted Boyfriend" resonate in various cultures, each adding its spin to the narrative. This cross-pollination of ideas creates a rich tapestry of global meme culture, where clichés are constantly redefined and re-contextualized.

The beauty of meme culture lies in its ability to take the mundane and elevate it to the extraordinary. Memes transform clichés into shared experiences, allowing people from all walks of life to connect over a shared laugh. They democratize humor, giving everyone a voice in creating and disseminating content. In this digital age, memes are the new storytellers, using clichés as their canvas to paint pictures of modern life that are as insightful as they are entertaining. Whether you're a teen scrolling through TikTok or a retiree exploring Facebook, memes offer a window into the collective consciousness of the internet, where clichés find new life and laughter is always just a click away.

Digital Storytelling: The Role of Clichés in Online Content

Picture the digital landscape as a sprawling library where *"Once upon a time"* isn't just a prelude to fairy tales but a jumping-off point for countless online narratives. Digital storytellers have embraced this classic beginning, weaving it into blogs, YouTube videos, and podcasts. It's a nod to the familiar, an invitation to suspend disbelief and dive into a tale that promises adventure, wisdom, or a good ol' chuckle. Creators use clichés like this to anchor their content, giving audiences a comforting sense of what's to come, even as they introduce twists that keep viewers on their toes.

Balancing originality with familiarity is the tightrope that digital creators walk daily. Take YouTube, where creators deftly juggle narrative formulas that echo traditional storytelling while adding unique flair. They might start with a cliché—like a classic *"fish out of water"* Scenario—but then layer in unexpected elements, like a pet ferret with a penchant for mischief. This blend of the expected and the novel keeps audiences engaged, offering the comfort of a known structure and the excitement of a fresh perspective. The trick lies in meeting audience expectations while subverting them just enough to spark intrigue and keep viewers coming back for more.

Familiarity is a powerful tool in digital storytelling, influencing how audiences connect with content. Clichéd story arcs, like the hero's journey or the rags-to-riches tale, resonate deeply because they tap into universal themes. Web series often lean on these tropes, providing viewers with a narrative road-map that feels fresh and predictable. This predictability encourages viewer retention, as audiences return for the satisfying progression of a story they intuitively understand. It's like re-watching a favorite movie—you know the beats, but you still relish the journey from start to finish. Familiarity breeds connection, offering a sense of belonging in the vast, often overwhelming digital world.

Yet, originality remains the holy grail for digital storytellers who strive to stand out in a sea of content. Avoiding clichés requires creativity and a willingness to push boundaries. One strategy involves re-imagining traditional tropes with a modern twist, like setting a classic love story in a virtual reality universe. Another approach is to infuse narratives with personal anecdotes or unexpected perspectives, providing a fresh take on well-worn themes. Techniques like these breathe new life into digital content, ensuring that even the most familiar stories feel dynamic and original. By challenging conventional narratives, creators can maintain their originality while still drawing on the timeless appeal of clichés.

Digital storytelling thrives on the interplay between the familiar and the new, where clichés serve as both a foundation and a springboard for innovation. They guide audiences into narratives that resonate on a deep level while leaving room for creative exploration. For creators, the challenge lies in weaving these elements together, crafting stories that capture the essence of "Once Upon a Time" while propelling them into uncharted territory. In the ever-evolving digital landscape, clichés provide a touchstone, a reminder that while the tools may change, the power of a good story remains eternal.

The Influence of Influencers: Clichés in Digital Branding

In the vast universe of social media, where everyone is a star in their own right, influencers have emerged as the constellations guiding trends and tastes. They've mastered crafting digital personas that resonate with their audiences, often relying on familiar phrases to make that connection. "Live your best life" has become the influencer's anthem, a rallying cry for self-empowerment and positivity. It's plastered across Instagram captions and YouTube vlogs, offering a feel-good message that resonates with followers. These clichés work because they tap into universal desires for happiness and fulfillment, acting as a digital pat on the back for those scrolling through their feeds.

The effectiveness of clichés in personal branding lies in their relatability. Influencers know that a well-placed motivational quote can be the digital equivalent of a warm hug. They sprinkle these phrases into their content like confetti, adding color and texture to their posts. Take Instagram, where influencers often use clichés to enhance their relatability. A simple "Good vibes only" post can rack up thousands of likes, as followers resonate with the message and the sentiment behind it. In video content, consistent catchphrases become part of an influencer's identity. These repeated phrases are like theme songs for their brand, instantly recognizable and closely associated with the person behind the screen.

However, relying too heavily on clichés can be a double-edged sword. While they foster relatability, they can also challenge brand authenticity. Sponsored posts, in particular, walk a fine line. When an influencer promotes a product with a generic phrase like "Must-have of the season," it can feel disingenuous, like a commercial masquerading as a personal recommendation. Followers are savvy; they can spot inauthenticity from a mile away. The balance between authenticity and cliché is crucial. Authentic influencers manage to weave sponsored content seamlessly into their narrative, maintaining trust with their audience while promoting a brand. It's about making sure the message feels natural, not forced.

Some influencers break the mold, offering fresh perspectives that subvert clichés rather than rely on them. These trailblazers aren't afraid to challenge the status quo, bringing a unique voice to the digital landscape. They might embrace humor, using witty commentary to poke fun at traditional influencer tropes. Or they might focus on niche content, appealing to audiences who crave something different from the norm. By breaking stereotypes and offering something novel, these influencers carve out a space for themselves, attracting followers who appreciate their originality. They prove that while clichés can be effective, there's immense value in authenticity and creativity.

In the world of digital branding, clichés are a tool—one that must be wielded with care. They offer a shortcut to connection, but they require a deft touch to avoid slipping into predictability. Influencers who master this balance can create content that resonates deeply with their audience, turning followers into loyal fans. The key lies in knowing when to lean into a cliché and when to step away, offering something fresh and unexpected. In doing so, influencers can maintain their authenticity while engaging with their audience meaningfully.

Navigating Miscommunication: Clichés in Text and Tweets

In this age of instant messaging and tweets, communicating with clarity can feel like trying to nail jelly to a wall. You send a text, and suddenly, you're caught in a whirlwind of misunderstanding. Why? Well, blame it on the digital clichés. A simple "It is what it is" might sound zen in your head, but online, it can be dismissive or even passive-aggressive. Text strips away tone, leaving words naked and vulnerable to misinterpretation. You think you're being straightforward, but your message might be as clear as mud to the recipient. The absence of vocal inflection and body language in digital communication means that clichés, which rely heavily on context, can easily lead to crossed wires.

Twitter, with its character limit, is a breeding ground for clichés. They say brevity is the soul of wit, but it's also the nemesis of nuanced communication. When you're limited to a scant number of characters, it's tempting to fall back on clichés. They're quick and easy, and they get the job done—or so you think. Phrases like "It is what it is" become crutches, used to convey a world of meaning in a handful of words. Yet, this reliance on brevity can dilute the message, reducing complex thoughts to simplistic statements that lack depth. It's like trying to paint a masterpiece with a roller instead of a brush.

Consider a few strategies to navigate the choppy waters of digital communication without hitting the cliché iceberg. First, aim for precision. Instead of leaning on well-worn phrases, try expressing your thoughts in clear, specific language. Cut through the noise with words that mean exactly what you intend. And when words fail, emojis can be your lifeline. Those little icons, once the domain of teenagers, now serve as essential punctuation in the text-based world. A winking face or a thumbs-up can add layers of meaning, clarifying tone and intent. They're the modern-day hieroglyphs, adding nuance and personality to otherwise flat text.

Digital clichés don't just affect communication; they can also impact relationships. Anyone who's been "ghosted" knows the gut punch of silence that follows a once-lively conversation. Ghosting, a term born in the digital age, has become a cliché. It's the ultimate non-response, a way of saying nothing, yet speaking volumes. When communication breaks down into clichés, it can erode the foundation of personal connections. Relying on superficial phrases can make interactions feel transactional rather than meaningful. It's like trying to build a relationship on a foundation of sand—the slightest wave, and it all comes tumbling down.

In the realm of digital interaction, clichés straddle the line between being a convenient tool and a potential pitfall. They serve as a quick fix, a linguistic shortcut for when time is of the essence or when the right words seem just unreachable. However, this convenience comes at a cost. There's a tangible risk of diluting rich, multifaceted conversations into mere collections of overused phrases. As we tread through the digital landscape, it becomes crucial to bear in mind that, although clichés can provide a sense of comfort and familiarity, they must not overshadow the authenticity inherent in genuine dialogue. The next time you find yourself poised to compose a text or construct a tweet, pause for a moment of reflection. Consider whether your chosen words truly convey your intended message, or if you're merely seeking refuge behind the all-too-convenient veil of digital clichés. This level of mindfulness might be the key to preserving the depth and integrity of our online communications, ensuring that they resonate with clarity and sincerity.

Chapter 6: Clichés in Business and Professional Life

Picture this: you're in a meeting, and someone suggests you "boil the ocean" to tackle a new project. You nod along, but inside, you wonder if you should grab a kettle or quietly exit the room. Welcome to the world of business jargon, where clichés roam free, turning every discussion into a game of buzzword bingo. It's a language that can make even the most straightforward conversation feel like deciphering an ancient code. While these phrases might give the illusion of savvy professionalism, they're often barriers to understanding, obscuring meaning like fog on a window.

Breaking the Mold: Avoiding Business Jargon

In the corporate world, jargon is as common as coffee stains on a break-room table. Terms like "synergy" and "think outside the box" are tossed around so frequently that they're practically the office wallpaper. But despite their prevalence, these clichés can hinder communication more than they help. When every meeting sounds like a jargon jamboree, clarity takes a back seat, leaving everyone nodding along while secretly wondering what on earth is being discussed. It's like trying to have a meaningful chat while someone plays the bagpipes in the background—distracting and ultimately unproductive.

So, how do you cut through the buzzword blizzard and get back to clear communication? Start with a jargon audit. This isn't as scary as it sounds—no need for a magnifying glass or detective hat. Just look at your internal memos, emails, and reports. Highlight those overused phrases that have become the verbal equivalent of elevator music. Once identified, it's time to rewrite them with clarity in mind. Instead of saying you'll "leverage synergies," try "collaborate." It's clearer and won't leave people reaching for a dictionary. Similarly, swap "push the envelope" for "innovate." It's direct and gets to the point without the paper-thin metaphor.

Jargon doesn't just obscure meaning; it can also create confusion, especially for those unaware. It's like trying to follow a recipe when you don't know what half the ingredients are. Buzzwords can leave people scratching their heads, wondering if they're the only ones who missed the memo. For those who have learned English as an additional language, jargon can be a double whammy, compounded by cultural references that fly overhead like low-flying aircraft. The result? Misunderstandings, decreased productivity, and a lot of head-scratching. It's like playing a game of telephone, where the message that started as "pass the salt" ends up as "fasten your seat belt."

But fear not! You can turn the tide by swapping out these confusing phrases for straightforward language. Instead of "aligning objectives," just say "agreeing on goals." It's simple and immediately understandable. Avoiding jargon means considering your audience and speaking directly, much like chatting with a friend over coffee rather than a board meeting with a thesaurus. When you cut through the jargon, you create an environment where everyone feels included, from the new intern to the seasoned executive. It's not just about making communication more efficient; it's about making it more human. After all, the goal is to connect, not to confound.

Jargon Detox Exercise

Dedicate time to carefully examine your most recent emails or reports. Identify and underline any instances of jargon or clichés that clutter your communication. Challenge yourself to rephrase these segments into straightforward, accessible language. For instance, transform "utilize operational synergies" into "work together more efficiently." Once you've refined your message, share this clearer version with a colleague. Ask for their feedback, specifically inquiring if the revised communication is more comprehensible. This hands-on practice sharpens your communication skills and contributes to cultivating an environment where clarity and collaboration are at the forefront. Engaging in this exercise regularly will enhance the quality of your interactions and encourage a workspace where everyone, regardless of their background or level of expertise, can contribute meaningfully and without misunderstanding.

The Power of Authentic Communication

In the bustling corridors of corporate life, where emails fly faster than paper airplanes and meetings stack up like pancakes at a breakfast buffet, authenticity can often feel like a unicorn—rare and elusive. Yet, genuine interactions are the secret sauce that turns a group of individuals into a cohesive team. Imagine a workplace where communication is as transparent as a freshly cleaned window. When leaders and team members communicate openly, trust flourishes. People feel valued and heard, knowing their opinions aren't just floating in the void like messages in a bottle. Transparent communication builds bridges, not walls, and creates an environment where everyone can thrive.

So, how do you foster genuine dialogue in a sea of corporate chatter? It starts with active listening. It's not just about nodding along like a bobblehead doll; it's about truly hearing what the other person is saying. Active listening means putting aside distractions, making eye contact, and responding thoughtfully. It's the difference between a conversation and a monologue. By listening actively, you show respect and foster an atmosphere where people feel safe to express themselves. And then there's the power of personal storytelling. Sharing your own experiences can create connections that go beyond spreadsheets and deadlines. It's like swapping tales around a campfire, where everyone leans closer. A well-told story can break down barriers, turning a room full of colleagues into a community.

Authenticity isn't just a feel-good concept; it has tangible benefits in the professional realm. When people communicate honestly, teamwork takes on a new level of cohesion. Imagine a crew rowing in perfect harmony, each person trusting the others to keep pace. That's what happens when openness prevails in the workplace. Collaborations become smoother, ideas flow more freely, and the team moves forward as a united force. Genuine communication fosters an environment where creativity can blossom and innovation can thrive. It's like adding a secret ingredient to a recipe, elevating the dish from ordinary to extraordinary.

Take a look at companies that have embraced authenticity and reaped the rewards. Take Patagonia, for example. Known for its commitment to transparency, this company doesn't just talk the talk; it walks the walk. Patagonia has built a loyal following and a strong internal culture by being upfront about its environmental impact and encouraging open dialogue. Employees feel empowered to voice their ideas and concerns, knowing they'll be met with respect and understanding. This approach has strengthened the company internally and enhanced its reputation globally. Another example is Zappos, where authenticity is woven into the fabric of the company culture. By valuing transparency and encouraging employees to be themselves, Zappos has created a workplace where people genuinely enjoy coming to work. The result? Happy employees, satisfied customers, and a thriving business.

Authenticity might not be the easiest path, but it's undoubtedly the most rewarding. In a world where facades often overshadow reality, genuine communication stands out like a beacon. It encourages trust, fosters collaboration, and turns the workplace into a place where people feel truly engaged. So, the next time you find yourself in a meeting or sending an email, remember the power of authenticity. It's not just about getting the job done; it's about lasting connections.

Engaging Presentations: Moving Beyond the Cliché

We've all been there—sitting through a presentation where the speaker drones on "low-hanging fruit" or drops an "at the end of the day" like it's confetti. These overused phrases are like the surprise raisins in a cookie that you thought was a chocolate chip. They distract rather than delight, turning what should be a riveting exchange of ideas into a snooze-fest. When every point is wrapped in clichés, the audience tunes out, missing the actual message. It's like trying to enjoy a song when all you can hear is static. To truly captivate an audience, you need to kick these verbal crutches to the curb and opt for content that resonates with originality and flair.

Creating a dynamic presentation is akin to producing a mini-theater performance—complete with a plot, characters, and maybe even a twist ending. Start by weaving storytelling techniques into your content. Picture yourself as the protagonist on a quest, with your audience along for the ride. The narrative arc should take them somewhere meaningful, not just through a list of bullet points. Speaking of which, ditch the bullet points whenever possible. They're the wallflowers of presentation slides—necessary but uninspiring. Instead, use storytelling to paint vivid mental pictures. Share anecdotes that bring your points to life, and your audience will hang on your every word, much like a captivated audience at a gripping play.

Interactive elements can turn your presentation from a monologue into a dialogue. Think of these elements as the karaoke machine at a party—suddenly, everyone's engaged. Pose questions to the audience and encourage them to share thoughts or experiences. Use polls or quizzes to break the ice and keep the energy flowing. When your audience becomes part of the conversation, they're more likely to stay focused and retain the information. It's like adding a little spice to a dish; it enhances the flavor and makes the meal a memorable experience. The goal is to create a memorable interaction where the audience feels like a valued participant rather than a passive recipient.

Visuals play a crucial role in presentations, acting as the supporting cast that enhances the main event. A well-placed info-graphic can do wonders, making complex data digestible and engaging. It's the difference between showing a map of the world and describing it. Infographics are like the visuals in a comic book—colorful, concise, and capable of telling a story all on their own. They catch the eye and convey information quickly, allowing you to communicate more with less. Let visuals do the heavy lifting instead of overwhelming your slides with text. They add depth to your presentation, making it both informative and visually appealing. When done right, visuals can leave a lasting impression, ensuring your message lingers long after the presentation ends.

Rehearsal and feedback, often overlooked, play pivotal roles in sharpening your presentation skills. Consider the analogy of baking a cake—without tasting the batter or checking the oven's temperature, the final product may fall flat. Similarly, rehearsing your presentation allows you to fine-tune your delivery, ensuring your message isn't just heard but felt by your audience. Start by practicing in an environment that simulates your actual presentation setting as closely as possible. This might mean standing up, using your presentation remote, and projecting your voice as if addressing a room full of people. Such rehearsals help you get comfortable with your content, manage your pacing, and refine your gestures, making your delivery appear effortless and engaging. Recording your practice sessions offers invaluable insights. By watching yourself, you can observe your body language, evaluate your tone, and pinpoint any distracting habits, such as pacing or overuse of "um" and "like." This self-review acts as a powerful tool, providing a clear picture of your strengths and pinpointing specific areas for improvement. Furthermore, seeking feedback from peers transforms the rehearsal process from a solitary exercise to a collaborative effort. Invite a mix of colleagues—those who are familiar with your work and others who might be encountering your subject for the first time—to serve as a test audience. Their diverse perspectives can uncover blind spots and offer constructive criticism that elevates your presentation. Encourage them to be candid, asking for feedback on clarity, engagement, and the persuasiveness of your arguments. Incorporate their insights into your practice, iterating on your delivery until it resonates clearly and compellingly. This iterative process, combining self-reflection with external feedback, ensures that when the moment comes to deliver your presentation, you're not just ready but primed to captivate and inspire your audience.

Leadership Language: Inspiring Through Originality

Leadership is like cooking; the right ingredients make all the difference. In the realm of leadership, language is that key ingredient. It's the seasoning that turns a bland dish into a memorable feast. A leader's words have the power to inspire, motivate, and unite a team. But when those words are bogged down by jargon, they lose their flavor. Effective leaders communicate with clarity, painting vivid pictures that capture the imagination and energize the spirit. Think of it as leading with vision, not jargon. You want your message to be as clear as a bell, ringing out across the room and leaving no doubt about the path forward.

Crafting impactful leadership messages requires both art and science. It's not just about what you say but how you say it. Start by developing a leadership narrative that resonates with your team. This narrative serves as your compass, guiding your words and actions. It should be authentic, aligning with your values and the goals of your organization. To convey your vision, use metaphors that bring abstract ideas to life. A well-chosen metaphor is like a snapshot for the mind, distilling complex concepts into relatable images. For example, describing a team as a "well-oiled machine" evokes a sense of efficiency and harmony. It's these vivid images that stick with people, making your message more memorable and impactful.

Consistency and sincerity are the twin pillars of effective leadership communication. Imagine a leader who elaborates on open-door policies but keeps their office door closed tighter than a drum. Words and actions must align; otherwise, the message crumbles like a house of cards. Authentic leaders lead by example, showing through their actions that they walk the talk. This alignment builds trust, creating an environment where team members feel valued and understood. It's about being genuine, not just delivering lip service. A leader's sincerity shines through when they communicate openly and honestly, acknowledging challenges and celebrating successes. This approach fosters a culture of transparency and trust, where everyone feels empowered to contribute their best.

Original language can drive cultural change within an organization. When leaders communicate innovatively, they challenge the status quo and inspire others to do the same. Transformational leadership through language means using words to ignite passion and creativity. It's about fostering an environment where new ideas are welcomed and encouraged. By speaking with originality and conviction, leaders can reshape the organizational culture, turning it into a dynamic and adaptive entity. This kind of communication invigorates the workplace, creating a culture that thrives on innovation and continuous improvement. It's like opening the windows to let fresh air in, revitalizing the atmosphere and sparking a renewed sense of purpose.

The impact of original language extends beyond the immediate team. It can ripple through the organization, influencing how employees interact, collaborate, and innovate. A leader who communicates with creativity and authenticity sets the tone for others, inspiring them to embrace new ways of thinking. This cultural shift can lead to breakthroughs and advancements, positioning the organization as a leader in its field. It's a ripple effect that begins with a single word, a single phrase, spoken with intention and purpose. By cultivating a language of originality, leaders can drive meaningful change, creating a legacy of innovation and success.

Networking with Nuance: Building Authentic Connections

Networking. The word alone can send shivers down your spine, conjuring images of awkward handshakes and forced smiles. But what if networking didn't have to feel like a dreaded chore, but rather like catching up with an old friend? This is where the magic of language comes into play. In the professional world, words can either build bridges or put up barriers. Take the classic "Let's touch base"—a phrase that rolls off the tongue with all the sincerity of a canned voicemail greeting. Such clichés are the fast food of conversation: quick, easy, and lacking in substance. They're the linguistic equivalent of a limp handshake, doing little to foster genuine connections.

To transform networking from drudgery to delight, ditch the clichés and aim for meaningful dialogue. Start with personalized communication, especially in follow-ups. Instead of sending a generic "Nice meeting you" email, mention something specific from your conversation. "I enjoyed hearing about your project on sustainable farming," packs more punch than a template response. It shows you were listening and genuinely interested, not just going through the motions. Another strategy is active networking through shared interests. Find common ground, whether it's a hobby, a passion for a particular cause, or even a mutual love of dad jokes. Shared interests make the conversation more engaging, turning it into a lively exchange rather than a monotonous monologue.

Authenticity in networking isn't just a fluffy feel-good concept; it has real-world payoffs. Genuine connections are like planting seeds in a garden. With a little nurturing, they grow into a supportive network that can lead to long-term success. When relationships are built on sincerity, they're more likely to stand the test of time. A strong network offers support, opportunities, and a wealth of knowledge. It's like having a team of cheerleaders rooting for you, ready to lend a hand when needed. This network becomes a pillar of strength throughout your career, providing guidance, encouragement, and sometimes a well-timed pep talk.

Consider the tale of Carla, a marketing whiz who built her career on authentic connections. Her secret? She listens more than she speaks and always follows up with a personal touch. Whether sending a thoughtful article or remembering someone's birthday, Carla's attention to detail sets her apart. Her network is a testament to the power of genuine connections, filled with people who value her sincerity and trust her implicitly. Then there's Raj, a tech guru known for his knack for forging authentic professional bonds. Raj has a talent for remembering the little things, like a colleague's favorite coffee order or a friend's passion for cycling. These small gestures create lasting impressions, making Raj's network a tapestry of genuine relationships woven with trust and mutual respect.

Networking, when done with nuance and authenticity, transforms from a dreaded task into a rewarding experience. It becomes a journey of discovery, where each interaction offers the potential for growth and learning. By focusing on genuine connections, you build a network that supports you, celebrates your successes, and helps you navigate the challenges of the professional world. It's not about collecting business cards like Pokémon; it's about cultivating meaningful relationships that enrich your life and career. So, the next time you find yourself at a networking event, forget the clichés, embrace authenticity and watch your professional relationships flourish.

The Art of Persuasion: Crafting Compelling Narratives

Picture this: you're in a marketing meeting, and someone proposes a story-driven campaign. You might wonder, "Are we selling a product or pitching a Hollywood blockbuster?" But there's a reason why storytelling works wonders in business persuasion. Narratives engage us on a level that spreadsheets and statistics simply can't touch. They're not just about reciting facts but weaving them into a tapestry that resonates emotionally. When done right, these stories become the backbone of successful marketing campaigns, drawing people in with a compelling narrative arc that sticks like a catchy song you can't get out of your head.

Crafting persuasive content is more than just slapping together a few anecdotes and calling it a day. It requires structure, much like building a sturdy house. Start with a solid foundation by outlining the key points you want to convey. This ensures your narrative has a clear beginning, middle, and end, guiding the audience through your message without leaving them lost in the weeds. Think of it as a guided tour, not a scavenger hunt. Then, layer in emotional appeal. Humans are emotional creatures, and tapping into that can make your message unforgettable. Whether it's a heartwarming story about how your product changed a life or a humorous tale that highlights a common frustration, emotions are the glue that holds a narrative together.

Of course, it's not all about tugging at heartstrings. Balance is crucial. Logic and emotion must dance together, each taking the lead at the right moment. Logical frameworks provide the scaffolding for your narrative, ensuring it holds up under scrutiny. They offer the evidence and rationale that support your claims, giving your story credibility. Yet, without emotional hooks, even the most logical argument can fall flat. It's like baking a cake without sugar—technically possible but not particularly enjoyable. The best persuasive content finds a sweet spot where emotion and logic intertwine, creating a narrative that's both convincing and compelling.

Successful companies have mastered this dance, using narratives to achieve their business goals. Take the iconic "Share a Coke" campaign by Coca-Cola. By replacing its logo with popular names, Coca-Cola crafted a story around personal connection. It wasn't just about selling a drink; it was about sharing moments. This narrative resonated with consumers on a personal level, turning a simple product into a symbol of friendship and community. Similarly, TOMS Shoes built its brand on the story of giving. For every pair of shoes purchased, another pair is given to someone in need.

This narrative of compassion and social responsibility struck a chord with consumers, transforming a shopping decision into an act of kindness.

By integrating storytelling into business communication, you can transform the mundane into the memorable. Narratives have the power to cut through the noise, capturing attention and inspiring action. Whether you're crafting a marketing campaign, delivering a presentation, or leading a team, storytelling is a tool that can elevate your message and amplify your impact. It turns data into dialogue, transforming dry facts into engaging tales that resonate on a human level. As you embrace the art of persuasion through narrative, remember that stories are not just about selling products or ideas; they're about connecting with people. So, next time you find yourself in the throes of crafting content, think beyond the bullet points and consider the power of a well-told story to drive your message home.

As Chapter 6 draws to a close, consider how the power of narrative weaves through the professional world, shaping everything from marketing strategies to leadership styles. The next chapter will delve into clichés in emotional and inspirational contexts, exploring how familiar phrases can either uplift or undermine our personal growth. Stay tuned for more insights into the world of clichés and their hidden potential for transformation.

Chapter 7: Clichés in Emotional and Inspirational Contexts

Ever found yourself in the self-help section of a bookstore, surrounded by titles promising to change your life in ten easy steps? You mosey on over, pick up a book, and, like clockwork, you see the phrase "Follow your dreams" staring back at you. It's the bread and butter of motivational speak, as predictable as your aunt's fruitcake at Christmas. But why do these clichés flood self-help literature like a busted pipe? It turns out they're comforting, like motivational slippers for your soul. They tell us what we want to hear: that anything is possible if we just dream big enough. Yet, as cozy as they are, these phrases often gloss over the nitty-gritty details of reality, leaving us with sugar without the spice.

We all know the golden nugget, "You can do anything you set your mind to." It's the pep talk equivalent of a double espresso, meant to energize us into action. But let's be real. Not everyone can become an astronaut or a rock star overnight, even if we set our minds to it. These clichés can feel like they're selling tickets to a movie that's already halfway through. They lack the depth needed to inspire genuine change, much like a motivational poster that looks great but doesn't exactly detail the steps to success. Real life isn't a one-size-fits-all t-shirt; it's more like a patchwork quilt, stitched together from bits of trial, and error, and a dash of persistence.

The problem with these glossy clichés is their one-size-fits-all mentality. They promise results without considering individual circumstances. It's like suggesting everyone should climb Everest when some of us are still getting winded on the stairs. For instance, instead of "Reach for the stars," why not "Take small steps every day"? It's less glamorous, sure, but it acknowledges that progress is often incremental. Or rather than saying "Follow your dreams," how about "Find what truly matters to you"? This shifts the focus from a nebulous concept to something tangible, a north star guiding you through the fog of indecision. These alternatives aren't just more practical; they respect the individual journey, recognizing that the path to success is as diverse as the folks walking it.

Authenticity in motivational content is like the difference between a homemade cookie and a store-bought one. You can taste the sincerity in every bite—or word, in this case. Personal anecdotes trump generic advice every time. When someone shares their unique story, it resonates on a deeper level. It's like being invited into their living room for a chat over tea, rather than being lectured in a sterile conference hall. Real-life experiences carry weight, grounding advice in reality. They show us that while the journey might be tough, it's also very much doable, with all its twists and turns. This authenticity inspires change, not through flashy slogans, but through genuine connection.

Exercise: Reflecting on Authentic Experiences

Grab a journal and jot down a moment when you faced a challenge and overcame it. What did you learn? How did it shape your path? Reflect on how this experience can guide you in the future. Use this reflection as a foundation for crafting your motivational message, one that speaks to your truth and encourages others with authenticity.

As we navigate the world of motivational speak, it's clear that while clichés offer comfort, they often lack the substance needed to inspire real change. Let's embrace authenticity, sharing stories that resonate and encourage us to find our paths, one step at a time.

Genuine Inspiration: Crafting Original Affirmations

Imagine you're at a crossroads in life, standing there with a map full of confusing clichés telling you to take the road less traveled or to follow the path of least resistance. It's enough to make you want to chuck the map and just wing it. That's where personalized affirmations come into play. Unlike clichés that offer cookie-cutter advice, affirmations are like those custom-made playlists that hit all the right notes. They resonate with your values and goals, acting as a compass that guides you through the fog. Start by reflecting on what truly matters to you. Is it creativity, stability, or connection? Whatever it may be, tailor your affirmations to align with these values. It's like building your mantra that speaks directly to your heart and mind, not someone else's idea of success.

Crafting affirmations is a bit like tailoring a suit—it needs to fit just right. You don't want to be swimming in a sea of generic phrases that don't quite resonate. Instead, focus on tailoring these affirmations to your challenges. Maybe you're tackling self-doubt or trying to muster the courage to leap. A well-crafted affirmation should address these specific hurdles, much like a coach giving you a pep talk before the big game. The beauty of personalized affirmations is their power to enhance self-belief and motivation. They're like a shot of espresso for your soul, providing that much-needed boost to push you forward. When your affirmations are personally relevant, they pack an emotional punch, making them far more effective than any off-the-shelf slogan.

Writing authentic affirmations is an exercise in self-discovery. Grab a journal and let your thoughts spill onto the page. Writing is a way to uncover personal truths, shedding light on what's truly important to you. It's like peeling back the layers of an onion, revealing the core of your desires and aspirations. Visualization exercises can also provide clarity. Picture your goals as if they've already been achieved, and describe how it feels. This mental imagery creates a vivid picture of success, making it feel more attainable. Think of it as daydreaming with a purpose, where each visualization strengthens your belief in your abilities.

Successful individuals often use affirmations as part of their daily routine. Take Serena Williams, for example. She uses affirmations to boost her confidence and focus, repeating positive statements that reinforce her capabilities. Her affirmations are not just words; they're a part of her mindset, a tool she uses to navigate challenges both on and off the court. Consider crafting an affirmation for yourself, like "I am capable and worthy of success." This simple statement can be a powerful reminder of your potential, a beacon guiding you toward your goals. It's not just about saying the words; it's about believing them and letting them seep into your consciousness until they become a part of who you are.

Exercise: Craft Your Affirmation

Pause for a moment and take a deep, reflective look at your current aspirations and the hurdles that stand in your way. Grab a pen and paper, and begin to articulate a personalized affirmation that mirrors the specifics of your journey. Infuse this affirmation with positive, forward-looking language that encapsulates not just your goals, but the essence of what you strive to become. Make it a daily ritual to recite this affirmation, allowing its potent message to deeply permeate your consciousness and steadily fuel your motivation.

Remember, affirmations serve as more than mere collections of words; they are the distilled essence of your deepest yearnings and the catalysts for your evolution. When you devote the time to meticulously sculpt these affirmations, embedding them with your unique intentions and dreams, you forge a potent instrument of self-empowerment. This process is about discarding the empty echo of clichés and, instead, harnessing the transformative power of language that resonates with the core of your being. Through this practice, you affirm your aspirations and embark on the path of profound personal metamorphosis. So, let go of the generic and the superficial, and embrace the profound impact of words that genuinely echo your soul's ambition.

Emotional Resonance: The Power of Storytelling

Picture yourself in a theater, the lights dimming as the storyteller takes the stage. With a few words, they transport you to another world, making you laugh, cry, or ponder life's mysteries. That's the magic of storytelling. Unlike a stale cliché, a well-told story evokes empathy and connects with your emotions. It's like a warm hug for your brain, making you feel understood and less alone. Personal stories have the unique ability to resonate because they're rooted in real experiences, not just abstract ideas. When someone shares their journey, it's like being invited to walk alongside them, experiencing their joys and struggles firsthand. This emotional connection is what makes storytelling such a powerful tool for inspiring and motivating people.

Crafting a compelling narrative involves more than just stringing words together. You need to build tension and resolution, creating a journey that keeps your audience on the edge of their seat. Think of it like a rollercoaster ride, with its soaring highs and stomach-churning drops. The thrill comes not just from the ride itself, but from the anticipation of what comes next. Using vivid sensory details can transport your audience right into the scene. Imagine describing a bustling market, the vibrant colors of fruits and spices, the chatter of vendors and customers, and the tantalizing aroma of freshly baked bread wafting through the air. These details paint a picture so clear that your audience can almost taste and smell it themselves. By engaging multiple senses, you make your story come alive, drawing your audience into the narrative and making it memorable.

Storytelling isn't just for novels or campfires; it's a powerful tool in motivational contexts as well. Consider TED Talks, where speakers use personal stories to share big ideas and inspire change. These talks move audiences because they combine the power of narrative with the speaker's unique perspective. One memorable example is Chimamanda Ngozi Adichie's talk on the danger of a single story, where she shares personal anecdotes to illustrate the impact of stereotypes. Through her stories, she challenges listeners to broaden their perspectives and embrace diversity. The effectiveness of storytelling in these contexts lies in its ability to break down complex ideas into relatable and digestible pieces. It's like turning a textbook into a conversation, where the audience feels engaged and invested.

When incorporating storytelling into inspirational content, it's crucial to balance narrative with message. The story should align with the key takeaways you want your audience to remember. Think of the narrative as a vehicle, carrying your message to its destination. To ensure authenticity and relatability, draw from your own experiences. Authentic stories resonate more deeply because they're grounded in truth. They're like the difference between a beautiful painting and a mass-produced print—one is unique and personal, while the other feels generic and distant. By sharing your journey, with all its ups and downs, you invite your audience to connect with you on a human level, fostering understanding and inspiration.

Finally, remember that storytelling is about more than just telling a tale; it's about creating an experience. Your audience should feel like they've been on a journey with you, learning and growing alongside your characters. Whether you're sharing a personal anecdote or crafting an elaborate narrative, your story should leave a lasting impact, sparking reflection and inspiring action.

Avoiding the Trap: Authenticity in Inspirational Quotes

Ever walked into a home where "Live, Laugh, Love" is emblazoned on every wall? It's the motivational mantra that's become as ubiquitous as coffee shop Wi-Fi. But have you ever stopped to ponder why it's so popular? This phrase, like many in the world of inspirational quotes, serves as a quick pick-me-up, a verbal shot of espresso for the weary soul. But here's the rub: it often delivers more froth than substance. These clichés are like fast food for the soul— quick, convenient, and instantly gratifying, yet they often lack the depth and nourishment needed to inspire lasting change. They saturate our lives, from social media feeds to the decor aisle in your local home goods store, offering comfort but not much else.

The real issue with these overused quotes is that they often lack the authenticity needed to make a genuine impact. They're like those generic, mass-produced paintings you find in hotel rooms—nice enough to look at, but not something you'd hang in your living room. True inspiration requires depth and sincerity, qualities that these clichés often gloss over in favor of popularity. It's the difference between a politician's campaign promise and a promise from a friend. One is designed to appeal to the masses, while the other is rooted in personal connection and truth. When crafting inspirational messages, the focus should be on creating content that resonates on a personal level, not just something that looks good on a T-shirt.

So, how do you create original and impactful quotes that truly resonate? Start by drawing from personal experiences and insights. Think about the moments in your life that have shaped you, the challenges you've overcome and the lessons you've learned along the way. These are the seeds from which authentic and meaningful quotes can grow. It's like writing a song; the best lyrics often come from a place of personal truth. Consider quotes that have stood the test of time, like Gandhi's "Be the change you wish to see in the world." This quote isn't just catchy; it's a call to action, urging us to live our values and make a difference. Or take Hemingway's "Courage is grace under pressure." It's a reminder that true bravery isn't about grand gestures but about maintaining composure in the face of adversity. These quotes resonate because they speak to universal truths, yet they're rooted in authenticity and personal experience.

Crafting quotes that stand out involves more than just stringing a few words together. It's about capturing the essence of a thought or feeling in a way that's both relatable and profound. One strategy is to focus on the specifics rather than the general. Instead of saying something broad like "Find happiness," consider a more nuanced approach like "Find joy in the everyday chaos." This offers more depth and acknowledges the complexity of life, making it more relatable to those who've experienced the whirlwind of modern existence. Authentic quotes should also invite reflection, prompting the reader to consider their own life and experiences. They should feel like a conversation with a wise friend, offering insights that linger long after the initial reading.

In a world flooded with clichés, the challenge lies in crafting messages that cut through the noise and speak directly to the heart. It's about moving beyond the superficial and embracing the complexity of human experience. By focusing on authenticity and depth, we can create quotes that inspire real change, offering guidance and encouragement in a world that often feels overwhelming. So, the next time you feel tempted to reach for a well-worn phrase, take a moment to dig a little deeper and find the words that truly resonate.

Language of Empathy: Communicating With Heart

Imagine you're talking to a friend who's having a rough day. You can see it in their eyes, and hear it in their voice. What do you say? How do you show that you get it, that you're there for them? Here's where empathy works, it's magic. Words are more than sounds; they're bridges, connecting hearts and minds. Empathy is like a soft cushion you offer someone to land on, a way of saying, "I've got you." It's about using language that shows understanding and support, wrapping your words in warmth and care. Active listening is key—tuning in to what's being said, rather than just waiting for your turn to speak. When you listen actively, you pick up on the nuances, the things unsaid. It's about being present, nodding along, and offering responses that show you're on the same wavelength.

Language that validates feelings can transform a conversation. It's the difference between saying "You're overreacting" and "I understand why you feel that way." The latter acknowledges the other person's reality, making them feel seen and heard. It's like giving their feelings a stamp of approval, saying, "Hey, your emotions are valid, and I'm here for it." Empathy isn't about resolving problems; it's about sitting with someone in their moment, sharing the weight of what they're carrying. Reflective listening and paraphrasing are tools that help in this process. By repeating back what someone has said, in your own words, you show that you've truly absorbed their message. It's like holding up a mirror, reflecting their thoughts and feelings to them, ensuring they know you're on the same page.

Using "I" statements can express empathy without casting blame. Instead of saying, "You always forget to call," try, "I feel worried when I don't hear from you." This shifts the focus from accusation to personal experience, fostering a more open and understanding dialogue. It's about sharing your perspective while inviting the other person to see things from your viewpoint. Empathetic language builds trust and connection, like planting seeds that grow into strong, unbreakable bonds. When you communicate with genuine concern, you create an environment where people feel safe and valued, a place where relationships can flourish. It's the foundation of any meaningful connection, whether with a friend, family member, or partner.

In practice, empathetic communication shines in various settings. Take counseling sessions, where therapists use empathy to create a safe space for clients to explore their emotions. They listen without judgment, offering understanding and support, and guiding individuals through their struggles.

In personal relationships, supportive conversations can make all the difference. Imagine a partner who listens deeply, offering words of comfort and reassurance. This kind of empathy strengthens the relationship, turning it into a sanctuary where both people feel nurtured and cherished. Empathy isn't just a skill; it's a way of being, a commitment to connecting with others on a deeper level. Whether in a therapy room or around the kitchen table, empathy has the power to transform interactions, bringing people closer and fostering love and understanding.

Personal Growth: Moving Beyond Clichés

Imagine you're on a quest for personal growth, armed with nothing but a map filled with vague clichés like "Find yourself" or "Live your truth." You might as well be trying to navigate with a paper airplane. These clichés, while catchy, can often feel like cryptic fortune cookies—full of promise but lacking in practical guidance. They offer a whisper of direction but leave you stranded on the shores of self-discovery, wondering what exactly it means to "find yourself." It's like being handed a key with no door in sight. These phrases suggest a journey without a road map, leading to a cycle of introspection that might feel more like spinning in circles than moving forward.

To genuinely embrace personal growth, you need more than just catchphrases. Think of it like building a house: you wouldn't start without blueprints and a plan. The same goes for personal development. Setting specific, achievable goals is your blueprint. Instead of aiming to "be happier," why not aim to practice gratitude three times a week? Or rather than deciding to "get fit," set a goal to walk 10,000 steps a day. These bite-sized steps transform abstract aspirations into tangible actions. They keep you grounded, much like tying a balloon to your wrist so you don't lose it to the wind. Reflecting on experiences is another valuable tool. It's like sifting through a treasure chest of memories, pulling out the lessons that shine the brightest. By examining where you've been, you gain insight into where you want to go and how to get there.

Tailored growth plans are the secret sauce that makes personal development truly effective. Generic advice is like a one-size-fits-all hat—good in theory, but in practice, it rarely fits anyone just right. Customizing growth strategies to fit individual needs acknowledges the unique tapestry of your life. Maybe you thrive with structure, or perhaps you prefer a little chaos to keep things interesting. The key is to find what works for you and embrace it. Think of it like a buffet: you don't have to pile your plate with everything; just choose what nourishes you. By focusing on personalized development, you create a path that resonates with who you are, not who someone else thinks you should be.

Consider the stories of individuals who have truly transformed themselves, not through clichés, but through personalized journeys. Take the example of a friend who faced job loss as an opportunity. Instead of succumbing to the pressure of "finding a new passion," they took a more pragmatic approach. They assessed their skills, networked within their industry, and pursued additional training. This methodical and personalized approach led them to a fulfilling career that aligned with their strengths. Or think of celebrated figures like Oprah Winfrey, who constantly reinvented herself by setting specific goals and learning from experiences. Their transformations weren't magic; they were the result of careful planning and self-reflection, a testament to the power of tailored growth.

Personal growth isn't about conforming to a set of clichés. It's about embracing the nuances of your journey and crafting a path that reflects your unique experiences and aspirations. By moving beyond the constraints of generic advice and focusing on personalized strategies, we can unlock true transformation. So as you step forward, remember to chart your course with intention, guided by the wisdom of your own story.

As we close this chapter on personal growth, remember that each step you take is part of a larger narrative. With the right mindset and tools, you can move beyond clichés, embracing a path that's as unique as you are. Stay curious, keep learning, and look forward to the next chapter of your journey.

Chapter 8 The Future of Clichés

Picture this: you're scrolling through social media, dodging cat videos and life hacks, when you stumble upon someone proclaiming the arrival of the "new normal." You've heard it a million times, yet it is popping up like a persistent game of whack-a-mole. The "new normal" has become as common as toilet paper shortages and Zoom calls with your boss's cat thanks to the pandemic. It's a prime example of how current events shape our language, crafting new clichés faster than you can say, "quarantine and chill." These phrases capture the collective experience, offering a linguistic snapshot of a world in flux.

In the throes of COVID-19, society birthed a plethora of pandemic clichés. "Cancel culture" emerged as a social phenomenon, reflecting a shift in how we hold individuals and institutions accountable. It's become a catchphrase for public shaming, like a digital scarlet letter, often debated and dissected in the public sphere. These expressions, born from cultural shifts, act as linguistic mirrors, reflecting the zeitgeist of our times. They serve as shorthand for complex societal issues, providing a common language to discuss and dissect them. Yet, like all clichés, they risk losing their impact as they become overused, turning once-powerful statements into background noise.

Technology, ever the catalyst of change, plays a significant role in cliché formation. Consider "Zoom fatigue," a term that encapsulates millions' digital exhaustion after countless virtual meetings. Much like a well-worn couch, this phrase captures the essence of a shared experience—one where we've all been trapped in pixelated boxes, gazing into the abyss of a never-ending video call. Technology-driven lifestyles foster new clichés as people navigate the digital landscape, creating expressions that resonate with our tech-saturated existence. These phrases reflect the intersection of language and innovation, highlighting how technology reshapes our communication.

Popular media fuels the spread of new clichés, crafting catchphrases that become cultural touchstones. Hit series and viral songs introduce phrases that quickly infiltrate our lexicon, like "Winter is coming" or "to infinity and beyond." These expressions, born from the creative minds of writers and musicians, tap into the cultural consciousness, becoming part of everyday language. They spread like wildfire, perpetuated by memes and social media, turning fictional worlds into shared realities. Yet, their rapid dissemination also accelerates their life cycle, leading to saturation and eventual decline. "Fake news," once a term reflecting media skepticism, is now diluted by overuse, reminding us how quickly language can evolve and lose its potency.

As we navigate these linguistic waters, observing how quickly new expressions rise and fall is fascinating. In a world dominated by instant communication and viral trends, clichés can go from fresh to stale in the blink of an eye. The speed of information exchange amplifies this process, with phrases spreading across platforms and cultures at lightning speed. It's a linguistic rollercoaster where new expressions emerge and fade rapidly. This fluidity challenges us to adapt, embracing the ever-changing language landscape while remaining mindful of the clichés surrounding us.

Reflection Section: Spotting Modern Clichés

Take a moment to reflect on the clichés you encounter daily. Which ones have become so ingrained that you hardly notice them? Are there phrases you use that might be teetering on the edge of overuse? Consider how these expressions shape your communication, and challenge yourself to find new ways to convey old ideas. Embrace the opportunity to refresh your language, exploring the rich tapestry of words at your disposal. After all, in a world where language constantly evolves, there's always room for creativity and originality.

In this whirlwind of linguistic evolution, clichés remain both a comfort and a challenge. They reflect our shared experiences, offering insight into our world's cultural shifts. Yet, as they proliferate, they risk becoming empty vessels, stripped of their original impact. As we continue to explore the future of clichés, we must navigate this delicate balance, embracing the power of language to connect, inspire, and transform.

Globalization and Language: Clichés Across Borders

Picture the world as a giant pot of cultural stew. As globalization stirs the pot, languages and phrases blend, creating a rich broth of shared expressions. This interconnectedness has given rise to words like "think global, act local," a mantra in international business that encourages blending global strategies with local nuances. It's like trying to sell sushi in Paris with a French twist. As companies expand across borders, they adopt this mindset, crafting messages that resonate globally while maintaining a local touch. This cliché captures the essence of globalization, where the regional and global dance together in a carefully choreographed waltz.

As cultures collide and intermingle, their languages follow suit. Imagine a world where idioms from different cultures merge into new clichés, much like a linguistic smoothie. The term "melting pot" is a metaphor for cultural exchange, describing societies where diverse elements blend to form a cohesive whole. In multicultural societies, idioms and expressions from various backgrounds come together, creating new phrases that capture the essence of this fusion. These linguistic hybrids offer a glimpse into how cultures influence one another, transforming traditional expressions into something fresh and exciting. It's a testament to the power of language to adapt and evolve in response to changing cultural landscapes.

In multilingual environments, language diversity plays a crucial role in the evolution of clichés. As people borrow and adapt phrases from other languages, new expressions emerge, reflecting the dynamic nature of communication. Consider how English has adopted terms like "savoir-faire" from French or "schadenfreude" from German, seamlessly integrating them into its lexicon. These linguistic borrowings enrich the language, providing nuanced ways to express ideas that might not have a direct translation. This borrowing process mirrors the cultural exchange happening on a larger scale, where languages absorb and adapt elements from one another, creating a tapestry of shared expressions.

Some clichés have transcended cultural boundaries to achieve universal recognition. "Carpe diem," a Latin phrase meaning "seize the day," has become a global motivational slogan, inspiring people from all walks of life to make the most of the present. This expression, rooted in ancient wisdom, has found new life across languages and cultures, serving as a reminder to embrace opportunities and live in the moment. Similarly, proverbs often undergo translation while retaining their core message, like the Chinese saying, "A journey of a thousand miles begins with a single step." These cross-cultural clichés offer a common language for shared human experiences, bridging gaps and fostering understanding.

Exercise: Exploring Your Linguistic Melting Pot

Reflect on the idiomatic expressions and phrases you frequently use that have journeyed across cultures to find a place in your daily dialogue. Consider how seamlessly they've woven themselves into the fabric of your communication, becoming nearly invisible threads in the larger mosaic of your speech. What do these borrowed phrases reveal about the diverse cultural influences that shape your perspective? Challenge yourself to delve into the origins of these foreign expressions. Investigate their histories, understand the contexts in which they were born, and consider the nuanced meanings they've acquired over time. This exploration is not just an academic exercise but a journey into the heart of human connection. It offers a chance to appreciate the rich tapestry of global languages and how they enhance our ability to express complex emotions and ideas. As the forces of globalization continue to draw the world closer together, the blending and adaptation of clichés are inevitable, contributing to a dynamic and ever-changing linguistic landscape. These expressions, forged in the crucible of cultural exchange, serve as windows into the collective human experience, bridging divides and fostering a sense of unity. They underscore the reality that, despite the diversity of our tongues, the essence of our experiences is shared. Across the vast expanse of our planet, these clichés resonate, forming a symphony of understanding that transcends geographical boundaries and linguistic barriers.

Predicting the Unpredictable: Future Clichés

Imagine a future where environmental slogans zip through conversations like bees in a flower garden. As climate change narratives become more urgent, phrases like "green is the new black" or "carbon footprint" might become as common as "breakfast of champions." These expressions could emerge from the growing need for sustainability, echoing the call to action present in every Eco-friendly campaign. As society grapples with heating temperatures and melting ice caps, expect to hear these phrases buzzing around like environmentally conscious gnats. They'll be everywhere, from office water cooler chats to spirited debates in coffee shops, as we collectively try to save the planet one recycled cliché at a time.

Space exploration is another field primed to launch new clichés into our everyday vernacular. With billionaires racing to the stars and Mars looking more like a destination than a dream, metaphors from space could soon orbit our language. Phrases like "shooting for the moon" might take on new life, perhaps evolving into "aiming for Mars" or "nearing the asteroid belt." As space tourism becomes less of a sci-fi fantasy and more of a reality, these cosmic expressions will likely pepper our conversations. Imagine using "in the vacuum of space" to describe a Monday morning meeting—suddenly, it sounds much more exciting.

Societal, technological, and cultural factors will shape the development of future clichés. Climate change will continue to influence how we elaborate on the environment, driving the creation of new slogans and sayings. Meanwhile, technological advancements will introduce phrases that capture the spirit of innovation, much like "the cloud," which has become synonymous with data storage. Cultural shifts, too, will play a role as societal values and norms evolve, bringing new expressions to the forefront. These factors will combine to shape the ever-changing language landscape, crafting clichés that reflect the times in which we live.

Generational shifts will also play a pivotal role in the emergence of new clichés. With their penchant for slang and meme culture, younger generations are already creating expressions that could become tomorrow's clichés. Think about phrases like "spill the tea" or "flex," which have taken social media by storm. As these youthful expressions gain traction, they may become part of the broader lexicon, passed down like linguistic heirlooms. With each new generation, the language evolves, bringing fresh expressions to the forefront while retiring older ones. This dynamic process ensures that clichés remain relevant, reflecting the changing tides of culture.

Specific sectors, like health and wellness, are especially ripe for cliché formation. As self-care becomes a cultural mainstay, expect to hear phrases like "mindful living" or "wellness journey" more frequently. These expressions capture the zeitgeist of a society increasingly focused on mental and physical health. In a world where yoga mats are as standard as morning coffee, and millions download meditation apps, it's no surprise that health-related clichés are rising. They offer a way to articulate the growing emphasis on balance and well-being, turning once-niche concepts into everyday language.

As we gaze into the linguistic crystal ball, it's clear that the future holds a treasure trove of potential clichés, each capturing a slice of contemporary life. Whether they emerge from the push for a sustainable planet, the allure of the cosmos, or the quest for personal wellness, these expressions will continue to shape our communication. They'll reflect our world, offering insight into our collective hopes, dreams, and challenges. So, as you navigate the evolving landscape of language, keep an ear out for the next big cliché—chances are, it's just around the corner, ready to make its mark.

The Role of AI: Automated Language and Clichés

Imagine this: you're chatting with a virtual assistant about the weather, and it replies with the ever-so-clichéd, "Looks like it's raining cats and dogs." You might chuckle at its attempt to be relatable, but it's a prime example of how AI influences language patterns. As AI systems become more sophisticated, they tap into vast databases of human communication, picking up phrases like a toddler learning to talk. But unlike toddlers, AI can repeat these phrases ad nauseam, turning once-charming clichés into linguistic wallpaper. It's like having a parrot that knows only one line from a Shakespeare play—impressive at first, but eventually, you might want to teach it something fresh.

The potential for AI to perpetuate clichés is immense, particularly in automated customer service scripts. Picture yourself calling a company, hoping for a human touch, only to be greeted by an AI spouting, "Your call is important to us." It's the digital equivalent of a shrug. These scripts, designed to streamline interactions, often rely on repetitive phrases that, while efficient, can lack the personal touch we crave. It's like being served a meal by a robot chef—it gets the job done, but where's the soul? The challenge lies in balancing efficiency and individuality, ensuring AI-driven communication doesn't become a conveyor belt of clichés.

The rise of AI in language raises critical ethical questions. How do we maintain originality and creativity in AI-generated content? Bias in AI language models is a significant concern, as these systems can inadvertently reflect the prejudices in the data they're trained on. It's a bit like teaching a robot to cook using only your grandma's recipes—it might make a mean lasagna, but it'll never innovate beyond what it knows. Ensuring that AI doesn't merely regurgitate existing clichés requires careful oversight, blending human creativity with machine efficiency. There's a delicate dance between embracing AI's potential and preserving the authenticity that makes human communication so rich.

Chatbots and virtual assistants are already reshaping the way we communicate. From Siri to Alexa, these AI-driven tools have become part of our daily lives, answering questions, setting reminders, and, occasionally, making us laugh with their quirky responses. They're like the digital sidekicks we never knew we needed, always ready with a witty quip or a helpful suggestion. Yet, as they become more integral to our interactions, the risk of cliché overload looms. Without careful programming, these assistants might become more than echo chambers, repeating the exact tired phrases until we tune them out entirely.

The future of AI and language is a fascinating frontier, teeming with potential and pitfalls. As we navigate this brave new world, we must remain vigilant, ensuring that AI enhances rather than diminishes our communication. It's like teaching an old dog new tricks, requiring patience, creativity, and a willingness to step outside the box. The goal is to harness AI's power while preserving the vibrancy and originality that make language uniquely human. In this dance between man and machine, the challenge is to find harmony, blending the best of both worlds to create something truly remarkable.

The End of an Era? The Potential Demise of Clichés

Imagine a world where clichés are as scarce as a quiet toddler. As the demand for originality in content creation grows, the reliance on these linguistic crutches is waning. Writers, marketers, and creators of all stripes are being called to step up their game. They are tasked with creating innovative and original messages, rather than simply recycling previous content. Audiences are hungry for new ideas, not reheated ones. In a world where everyone has a platform, standing out means ditching the old clichés to favor something with a bit more pizzazz. It's like swapping out bell bottoms for skinny jeans—you've got to keep up with the times if you want to stay in fashion.

This cultural shift towards authenticity is not just a fad; it's a full-blown movement. People crave genuine expression like a dog craves belly rubs. Personalized marketing strategies are all the rage as companies strive to connect with audiences on a deeper, more meaningful level. The days of one-size-fits-all messaging are as outdated as a floppy disk. Today's consumers want to feel seen and heard, not lumped together with the masses. Successful brands speak directly to their audience's unique experiences, using language that resonates personally. It's no longer enough to toss out a generic "Have a nice day"; audiences would like to know you mean it.

Meanwhile, the rise of digital literacy is reshaping how people perceive clichés. With a world of information at their fingertips, audiences have become savvy content consumers. They can spot a tired phrase from a mile away like a parent spotting their child's attempt to sneak a cookie. This critical consumption means clichés are less effective at slipping by unnoticed. People are more discerning, demanding content that engages their minds rather than falling into autopilot. It's a wake-up call for anyone who relies on well-worn expressions to get their point across. The discerning audience will not be deceived by smoke and mirrors; they seek substance and clarity.

Movements promoting linguistic diversity are also gaining traction, encouraging people to embrace varied and innovative language use. Language preservation programs work tirelessly to keep lesser-known dialects alive, like a librarian guarding a collection of rare first editions. These initiatives celebrate the richness of linguistic diversity, encouraging unique expressions that reflect the tapestry of human experience. It's a push towards a world where language is as varied and vibrant as a field of wildflowers. As people explore the full range of linguistic possibilities, clichés lose their grip, making way for fresh, innovative communication methods.

Language, much like fashion, is ever-evolving. As society shifts towards originality, authenticity, and diversity, clichés risk becoming relics of the past. They served their purpose, like training wheels on a bike, but the time has come to ride free. The future of communication promises a landscape where every word counts and expressions are as unique as the individuals who use them. Whether you're crafting a message for a global brand or just trying to sound interesting at a dinner party, the call is clear: break free from the confines of cliché and embrace the endless possibilities of language.

A New Beginning: Embracing Change in Communication

Imagine a world where language is as dynamic and colorful as a chameleon at a disco. With the emergence of new communication technologies, we're on the brink of a linguistic renaissance. Think about it: we're no longer limited to pen and paper or screens. We've got virtual reality and augmented reality, and who knows what reality will come next? These technologies are changing how we interact, making language more fluid and adaptable. Suddenly, we're not just reading words; we're experiencing them in 3D, with full surround sound. It's like turning a black-and-white TV into a high-definition extravaganza. This shift opens up a playground for language, where creativity and innovation can thrive.

Creativity is the secret sauce in this evolving landscape. Sure, you could stick to the traditional, but where's the fun in that? Encouraging creative writing and expression is crucial for shaping the future of communication. Why settle for the same old when you can cook something new and exciting? As artists experiment with colors and textures, writers can play with words and styles, pushing boundaries and exploring uncharted territories. It's all about embracing the unknown, like a culinary explorer venturing into the wilds of flavor. The more we encourage creativity, the richer our language will become, offering fresh perspectives and unique expressions that keep us engaged and inspired.

Diversity is another ingredient in this linguistic recipe. By integrating diverse voices, we enrich language development, reflecting our varied experiences and backgrounds. Representation in media and literature is vital. It's like adding spices to a dish—each brings something different, transforming the ordinary into the extraordinary. By including diverse perspectives, we create a tapestry of language that resonates with a broader audience. It transforms into a living, breathing entity that evolves with us, encapsulating the essence of our identity and future direction. The more inclusive we are, the more vibrant and dynamic our language will be, offering a chorus of voices that sing harmoniously.

Fostering originality in language requires a culture that celebrates uniqueness and innovation. Workshops and educational programs can promote creativity, allowing people to experiment and play with language without fear of judgment. Imagine a classroom where students are encouraged to invent new words, craft poetry, and write stories that defy convention. It's like a laboratory for language, where the only limits are those of the imagination. By nurturing this environment, we cultivate a generation of thinkers and creators who see language not as a set of rules to follow but as a canvas upon which to paint. This approach ensures that our communication evolves in exciting and unexpected ways, keeping us on our toes and eager for more.

In this brave new world of communication, the possibilities are endless. We're standing at the threshold of a linguistic revolution, with the latest technologies and creative approaches leading the charge. We can transform our language into something remarkable by embracing change and encouraging originality. It's an exciting time to be a part of this evolution, with each of us contributing to the tapestry of human expression. Whether you're a poet, a programmer, or someone who loves a good pun, there's room for you in this ever-expanding conversation. So, let's dive in, explore the possibilities, and see where this journey takes us.

Conclusion

Well, here we are at the end of our delightful escapade through the world of clichés. It's been quite the journey, hasn't it? We've traveled from the ancient hills where clichés were birthed to the wild and wonderful digital age where they've mutated into memes and hashtags. We've peeked into the pages of Shakespeare and Dickens, laughed with comedians twisting old sayings into belly-aching punchlines, and even tried to replace stale phrases with fresh metaphors. It's been a rollercoaster of words and wit to make sense of these linguistic gems we call clichés.

Let's pause and reflect on why we've ventured into this quirky realm. Clichés, for all their familiarity, are powerful little beasts. They bridge the gap between generations and cultures, acting like the comforting macaroni and cheese of language. Yet, they can also stifle creativity, like a rain cloud hovering over a picnic. In this balancing act, clichés both unite us and hold us back. They are the old friends we love to hate, reminding us of shared experiences while challenging us to think anew.

So, what should you take away from all this linguistic exploration? First, clichés are more than just tired expressions—they are deeply woven into our daily lives, from casual chit-chat to global dialogues. Recognizing their role helps us appreciate and question our communication habits. More importantly, it pushes us to be better storytellers, to craft original expressions that light up our conversations like fireworks on the Fourth of July.

With this newfound insight, I invite you to embrace originality. Let's be honest: The world doesn't need another "at the end of the day." What it craves are fresh perspectives and creative spins that make people stop and think. Challenge yourself to swap out those worn-out phrases for something vibrant and new. It could be as simple as replacing "think outside the box" with "break the mold like a soufflé escaping its dish." Your language is your playground—so go wild!

And here's a little call to action to keep you on your toes. Experiment with your words. Play around with storytelling techniques, or invent a new turn of phrase. You might even want to keep a notebook of your favorite cliché alternatives. Who knows, you could be the next wordsmith to coin a phrase that everyone's quoting.

As we close this chapter, remember that language is ever-evolving. Keep an eye on emerging trends and be ready to adapt. There's always something new to learn, whether it's the latest viral meme or a new cultural idiom. Be curious, be daring, and let your words flow like a river carving its path.

On a personal note, this journey has been as enlightening for me as I hope it has been for you. Understanding clichés has shown me the transformative power of language. It's like discovering a secret ingredient that elevates a dish from ordinary to extraordinary. I'm grateful for your company along this whimsical ride through the world of clichés.

So, thank you for joining me on this adventure. I truly appreciate your willingness to explore and rethink these familiar phrases. Remember, the central message of our book is simple yet profound: By understanding and creatively engaging with clichés, we can enrich our communication and deepen our appreciation for the nuances of language.

Now, go forth and let your words dance to the rhythm of originality. And who knows, maybe one day, you'll be the one coining the next great phrase that becomes a cliché of its own. Keep exploring, keep creating, and most importantly, keep having fun with language.

The End

A WHIMSICAL JOURNEY THROUGH
THE WORLD OF CLICHÉS
The End
A WHIMSICAL JOURNEY THROUGH THE
WORLD OF CLICHÉS

P.S. The last thing I want to ensure is that I give a big SHOUT OUT & THANKS to all those who encouraged me to be the best version of me and never gave up on me. To my family and friends: Thanks for the journey! I live by this: 'Never give up; you never know what's around the other side.' Ready for the next adventure? I am! Hope to see you all there!

References

- *the oral tradition and its influence in the Greek and Roman ...* https://bmcr.brynmawr.edu/1999/1999.05.07/
- *The Origins of 8 Literary Clichés* https://www.mentalfloss.com/article/653302/literary-cliche-origins
- *Plato and Nietzsche: Their Philosophical Art | Reviews* https://ndpr.nd.edu/reviews/plato-and-nietzsche-their-philosophical-art/
- *Folklore and the Collective Unconscious: The Mythological ...* https://www.therattlecap.com/post/folklore-and-the-collective-unconscious-the-mythological-connection-between-disparate-cultures
- *In new cognitive research, people's eyes reveal that clichés ...* https://www.princeton.edu/news/2021/10/20/new-cognitive-research-princeton-peoples-eyes-reveal-cliches-are-underrated
- *Bridging Cultures: Understanding the Role of Clichés in ...* https://www.youtube.com/watch?v=pzr3FOh4E7o
- *Memes In The Digital Age: A Sociolinguistic Examination ...* https://kuey.net/index.php/kuey/article/download/5520/3874/11416
- *Two Candidates. Two Speeches. One Cliché After Another ...* https://www.nytimes.com/2016/06/10/us/politics/trump-clinton-speeches.html
- *The Science of Humor Is No Laughing Matter* https://www.psychologicalscience.org/observer/the-science-of-humor-is-no-laughing-matter
- *George Carlin's Foolproof System of Organizing Comedy ...* https://time.com/4949766/george-carlin-joke-system/
- *Does Ellen DeGeneres adopt rhetorical strategies in her ...* https://www.jlls.org/index.php/jlls/article/view/3511
- *The Translation of Humor and Its Challenges* https://terratranslations.com

/2021/03/24/the-translation-of-humor-and-its-challenges/

- *Writing 101: What Is a Cliché? Learn When to Use Clichés in ...* https://www.masterclass.com/articles/writing-101-what-is-a-cliche-learn-when-to-use-cliches-in-writing-and-20-common-cliches-all-writers-should-avoid
- *Writing exercises to spark your creativity - Dave McCreery* https://davemccreery.co.uk/writing-resources/writing-exercises/
- *Exploring the Impact of Figurative Language in Literature* https://www.researchgate.net/publication/378855245_The_Power_of_Metaphor_Exploring_the_Impact_of_Figurative_Language_in_Literature
- *Hemingway's Writing Style* https://www.cliffsnotes.com/literature/h/hemingways-short-stories/critical-essay/hemingways-writing-style
- *The Impact of Social Media on Language Evolution* https://www.researchgate.net/publication/382186538_The_Impact_of_Social_Media_on_Language_Evolution
- *The 21 Most Defining Memes of 2023* https://www.rollingstone.com/culture/culture-lists/best-memes-2023-1234918358/
- *The Role of Hashtags on Social Media* https://www.linkedin.com/pulse/role-hashtags-social-media-igrowmarketing
- *Authenticity in Influencer Marketing - Why It's Important* https://goatagency.com/blog/influencer-marketing/authentic-influencer-marketing/
- *How Corporate Jargon Hurts Communication in the Workplace* https://alis.alberta.ca/succeed-at-work/manage-challenges/how-corporate-jargon-hurts-communication-in-the-workplace/
- *4 powerful examples of effective leadership communication* https://slack.com/blog/collaboration/effective-leadership-communication-examples
- *8 Classic storytelling techniques for engaging presentations* https://blog.sparkol.com/8-classic-storytelling-techniques-for-engaging-presentations
- *The Power of Networking: How to Build Authentic ...* https://medium.com/@elliotmortenson/the-power-of-networking-how-to-build-authentic-connections-for-career-and-personal-growth-952a6dec4e66
- *The Worst Self-Help Clichés (My Top 5)* https://thehabitfactor.com/worst-self-help-cliches/

- *Creating Personalized Affirmations: A Step-by-Step Guide* https://www.abfc.co/creating-personalized-affirmations-a-step-by-step-guide/
- *The Art of Storytelling in Public Speaking* https://voiceplace.com/art-storytelling-public-speaking/
- *Authentic Quotes* https://www.brainyquote.com/topics/authentic-quotes
- *Pandemic clichés and how to avoid them* https://readable.com/blog/pandemic-cliches-and-how-to-avoid-them/
- *Language and Globalization* https://www.languagesunlimited.com/language-and-globalization/
- *AI and Linguistic Evolution: The Digital Catalyst in Language …* https://medium.com/@vennyturner/ai-and-linguistic-evolution-the-digital-catalyst-in-language-dynamics-bf4930b319d2#:~:text=As%20AI%20systems%20become%20more,even%20introducing%20new%20grammatical%20structures.
- *The Future of Communication Technology: Top Trends to …* https://frtinc.com/the-future-of-communication-technology-top-trends-to-watch/

About the Author

There, he [Brian] embraced diverse experiences, honing his skills in various roles – from dedicated housekeeping to leading maintenance operations at Quicksilver and even venturing into the world of ski school and private lessons in Breckenridge, Colorado. He cultivated a fearless spirit as a snowboarder, pushing his limits on the slopes. This adventurous spirit led him to pursue further education, earning a degree as a Physical Therapist Assistant. He then joined forces with his mother, Kristina L. Sommerkamp, in the world of finance, initially navigating the terrain of insurance, health, life, and annuities. However, Brian soon realized that his true calling lay in education, not sales, though he dutifully fulfilled his role. He embraced various healthcare-related positions, finding immense satisfaction in caring for others and bringing joy into their lives – a sentiment he hopes to mirror with his book. He eagerly awaits your feedback and encourages you to leave a review.

P.S. - Last thing I want to make sure is that I give a big SHOUT OUT & THANKS to all those that encouraged me to be the best version of me and to never give up! To my wife, my family and friends: Thanks for the journey! I live by this Cliche every day: 'Never give up, you never know what's around the other side.' Ready for the next adventure? I am! Hope to see you all there!

You can connect with me on:
 https://www.facebook.com/brian.bradley.18007